"Blake… I don't  **but I want to kis** **be kissed *by* you.** **lips seductively.**

He stood still, fighting the need to haul her into his arms and kiss them both senseless. Damn but he wanted her. All the way. So he had to leave. Except he couldn t. He always walked away. He'd left family and friends to hide his guilt, to start over. He'd held back with women for fear he'd hurt them, or be hurt. Which he could do to Georgie. But not if he gave her everything he had.

Her hand fell away. "I get the picture."

Blake reached for her, pulled her up close, lowered his mouth to hers. "No, you don't." Kissing Georgie was like falling into a cushion of air. Warm, hot, sensational, exhilarating. And most of all, Georgie was putting him back together again. All the doubts he'd carried for so long were evaporating. "Georgie," he whispered before plunging his tongue into her warmth to taste, to feel, to know her.

Dear Reader,

How does someone recover from losing their brother? Or their best friend?

Georgie Price and Blake Newman have struggled with grief and guilt for thirteen years, and when they next meet, it is because Blake's mother is seriously ill and he's frantic about what lies ahead for him and his family. Georgie thinks she's there to support this man from her past, but when they get together for the first time since the tragedy that wrecked their dreams, neither is prepared for the ease between them and the tenderness that quickly turns to heat and longing. But will it become love?

I hope you enjoy following Blake and Georgie's story. I loved writing it.

All the best,

Sue MacKay

FLING WITH HER LONG-LOST SURGEON

———

SUE MacKAY

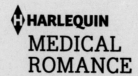

HARLEQUIN

MEDICAL
ROMANCE

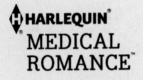

HARLEQUIN®
MEDICAL
ROMANCE™

Recycling programs
for this product may
not exist in your area.

ISBN-13: 978-1-335-73725-0

Fling with Her Long-Lost Surgeon

Copyright © 2022 by Sue MacKay

For questions and comments about the quality of this book,
please contact us at CustomerService@Harlequin.com.

Harlequin Enterprises ULC
22 Adelaide St. West, 41st Floor
Toronto, Ontario M5H 4E3, Canada
www.Harlequin.com

Printed in U.S.A.

Sue MacKay lives with her husband in New Zealand's beautiful Marlborough Sounds, with the water on her doorstep and the birds and the trees at her back door. It is the perfect setting to indulge her passions of entertaining friends by cooking them sumptuous meals, drinking fabulous wine, going for hill walks or kayaking around the bay—and, of course, writing stories.

Books by Sue MacKay

Harlequin Medical Romance

Queenstown Search & Rescue

Captivated by Her Runaway Doc
A Single Dad to Rescue Her
From Best Friend to I Do?

London Hospital Midwives

A Fling to Steal Her Heart

The Nurse's Twin Surprise
Reclaiming Her Army Doc Husband
The Nurse's Secret
The GP's Secret Baby Wish
Their Second Chance in ER

Visit the Author Profile page
at Harlequin.com for more titles.

To all my readers, thank you.
I'd be lost without you.
Cheers, Sue MacKay

**Praise for
Sue MacKay**

"Overall, Ms. MacKay has delivered a really good read in this book where the chemistry between this couple was strong; the romance was delightful and had me loving how these two come together."
—*Harlequin Junkie* on
The Italian Surgeon's Secret Baby

CHAPTER ONE

GYNAECOLOGIST GEORGINA PRICE stepped out of her office at Scott's Women's Health and tried not to stare at the man pacing the small space between her and the waiting room. Wow. Had he grown up or what? She'd never looked twice at him before, but then she was four years older than Blake and when he and her brother were knocking around together the last thing she'd been interested in was some pain in the backside who needed to grow up and get a life. 'Hello, Blake. It's been a long time since we last caught up.'

Thirteen years had turned the boy into an outstanding-looking man. She couldn't help but observe how the skinny young guy she'd last seen when she was twenty-three had become almost unrecognisable. Almost. The long, too-lean body had filled out in all the right places to become that of an attractive man. Stunning said it all— even when his once open face was now shuttered with lines tugging at the corners of his mouth and eyes. Sadly those eyes had lost their cheeky twinkle, but on the good side, the riotous curls were as dark and thick as ever, and still wild despite an upmarket haircut. As though the wind had been blowing through his hair on the way here. Oh, to run her fingers over his scalp, to feel the softness of those shiny curls. Her mouth dried. Definitely gorgeous.

Georgie, get a grip. Blake's here because of Sarah, nothing else.

His mother was very ill and had been referred to this practice for surgery. She'd wanted Georgie to be her consultant but understood it wasn't possible for ethical reasons as they were family friends. Georgie had seen to it that Andrew, a senior partner here, stepped up for Sarah, and right now Blake's mother was in with him going over tomorrow's procedure.

'I wish we were catching up in better circumstances.' Blake had stepped closer and, with a glance in the direction of the office where his mother was sitting patiently waiting for him to join them, said quietly, 'Is Mum putting on a brave face? Or are you the one she tells all to? Downloads on? I know she's talked to you a lot about what's going on.' He was hurting, and worrying himself sick. It was there in the dark gaze now locked on her as though she could alleviate his pain with a few words.

Not possible, sorry, Blake.

But as a doctor, he knew that. Georgie sighed. Later, when this was over and hopefully Sarah was back on her feet, he could return to being her late brother's best friend whom she hadn't seen since the funeral, but for now his mother was ill and preparing for major surgery tomorrow morning to remove a massive fibroid, as well as have a full hysterectomy because of the possibility of cancer. 'She's being Sarah, resilient and quiet.' And worried sick, but Georgie wasn't putting that into words. Blake sounded apprehensive enough as it was. Something she understood too well. While logically she and Andrew were ninety per cent certain Sarah didn't have a malignancy, the family friend part of her mind was afraid she might be wrong. The thought of this family being hurt gripped her, making her almost relieved she wasn't the one doing the surgery. She now understood better why Blake had felt so guilty over Noah's death when he had no reason to.

Blake shook his head. 'What else did I expect?' he muttered almost to himself.

'It would be more upsetting if she was behaving any different.'

Dull eyes met her full on. Where was that twinkle when she needed it? Because she also felt out of sorts about what Sarah and her family were facing. 'You're right. But sometimes I want to be the strong one.'

'You were always strong, Blake.' He'd never faltered when his cricket team needed runs from him, when her brother wanted to try some outlandish feat like leaping out of a plane wearing nothing but a parachute. He'd stepped up and passed his exams with the highest scores ever seen at the medical school he was trying to get into while he'd been broken-hearted over Noah's passing. He was tough. Or he had been. What did she know these days? Anything could've changed within him. She only had his mother's take on things now and of course Sarah would be biased, or unwilling to talk about anything distressing about her son, but reading between the lines, Georgie had a feeling Blake had struggled at times over the intervening years since all their lives had been changed for ever.

'You don't know the half of it,' Blake said quietly, verifying her own thoughts. 'But thanks for the vote of confidence.'

Andrew's door opened and he appeared. 'Like to join us, Blake?'

Blake swallowed. 'Sure.'

Georgie tapped his arm. 'Go on. You can do this. I'm available if you need to talk later.' Naturally she'd be there for this family that had been there for hers thirteen years ago.

He smiled tiredly. 'Thanks, Georgie. I might take you up on that.'

'Georgie,' Andrew called. 'Sarah would like you in on this too. As a friend,' he added pointedly. The direction of his gaze suggested that was more for Blake's sake than hers.

But Blake didn't hesitate. He held out his

hand and gestured to the doorway. 'After you, Georgie.'

Ever the gentleman. 'Thanks.' It was easy to smile at him as she went past. Strange how right it felt being here with him.

Sitting down at his desk, Andrew quickly filled them in on details. 'I've explained the operation to Sarah, and also made it very clear that she has to take things easy for the following six weeks.'

'Good luck with that.' Blake squeezed his mother's shoulder, a grim look on his face. 'I'd like to see the X-ray and scans that were taken of this fibroid.'

Andrew nodded. 'Your mother said you'd want to do that. I totally understand, especially being a doctor.'

Standing by the door, Georgie glanced beyond the chair where Sarah sat to the man she hadn't seen for so long and once more took in his good looks, strong chin and the determination in those eyes that always used to be filled with laughter and fun. A lot like hers before her brother's accident. Now she saw pain and fear, presumably brought on by his mother's illness and knowing what it was like losing someone special. Had his life been all he'd once hoped for? From the little she'd heard from Sarah, apart from his medical career, he didn't seem to have followed through on anything else he might've dreamed about, like marrying and having a family. But maybe he hadn't found the right woman yet, or was too busy protecting his heart to get involved with someone who might cause him hurt again.

Sounded awfully familiar, she conceded. There'd been a few failures along the way for her. It was possibly the same with Blake. They'd both hurt badly over Noah, and she'd lost a lot of confidence and trust, so why wouldn't it be? She had tried to let go the pain of losing Noah, had even fallen in love and married, only to end up divorced and sorry for the pain she'd put her husband through. Afraid of the consequences if something terrible happened to him, she hadn't been able to give him enough love. Especially after she lost their baby at twelve weeks. That had been the final straw. More pain, more loss, and it made her feel guilty for even trying for happiness when Noah would never experience those things. She'd withdrawn from looking for love and a family, and got on with what she was good at by putting her heart and soul into it—medicine.

Which made the way she was noticing Blake as an attractive man rather odd. She hadn't felt any warm tingly sensations tickling her since her marriage fell apart. It had to be more to do with catching up with someone who'd known her brother so well and understood the pain of losing him than anything else.

Sarah was talking, reminding Georgie why she was here. 'Blake.' Sarah paused until she had her son's full attention. 'Andrew's my specialist and he doesn't need any input from you. You're not the doctor in this situation. You're my son.' She reached for his hand and gave him a mother's smile. Gentle, understanding and 'do as you're told' all rolled into one.

Georgie's heart expanded, and her eyes watered. Family love was so enveloping and got a person through the daily hits life sent. Her parents gave her strength and understanding, as well as acceptance: things she'd needed over the years, and still did occasionally. She thought of Sarah and knew

Blake had been given all the support he needed, but had he accepted it?

'Andrew won't take the slightest bit of notice of anything Blake says anyway.' Georgie smiled at the woman she'd known for as long as she had Blake, which was since he and Noah met at the private school they'd attended here in Christchurch and became inseparable when it came to getting into mischief. Over time their families had got to know each other, but she hadn't had a lot to do with the boys as the age gap had seemed huge back then. But in the intervening years she had got to know Sarah and Alistair, Blake's dad, quite well over dinners at her parents' place.

'Nor would you.' Blake had found it in himself to smile at her for the first time since she'd set eyes on him. He did still appear uncomfortable with being here though. It was a scary time for him and his family with the cancer question hanging over them like a black cloud in an otherwise bright blue sky. Memories of pain from the past would up the stress levels and tighten those well-shaped shoulders even further.

Blake and Noah had been in their second

year at university in Dunedin when tragedy struck, taking Noah from them. Blake had not coped with losing his best mate and blamed himself for the accident that killed him, when it couldn't be further from the truth. He'd believed if he'd been with Noah that night, he'd have prevented him from getting into the car with the drunk driver. Since then Blake had been notable by his absence in Christchurch, and rarely visited her parents on the few occasions he did spend a few days with his family. She knew Sarah and Alastair struggled with his absence but they also understood and supported him. It was as though they too had lost a son the same night her parents lost Noah.

'Yes, I still like to be in charge,' she admitted. 'I'm guessing you do too.' It was a way of surviving. But in this case Blake wasn't a gynaecologist or obstetrician so his mother's condition was out of his league. His strength was in orthopaedics—which would only make this more frightening. There was nothing he could do but wait and be there for his parents and sisters. Returning his smile, Georgie felt awkward. It was true they hadn't been close but he'd been around her family a lot as a teenager, like a part of the furniture, as had her brother with Blake's family. Now he was worried for his mother, and so was she, even when, from what she'd seen and talked through with Andrew, medically she believed Sarah did not have cancer. It would only be once the surgery was done and Andrew could say with some certainty there was no cancer would she begin to relax. Even then it would take a negative pathology report to take away any lingering doubts.

Sarah looked from her son to Georgie, and back. 'Even though I understood Georgie couldn't be my specialist I rang her the moment I knew I had to have this operation. I want her close to the action.'

Georgie nodded and smiled at Blake. 'Your mother rang me at home while I was enjoying a quiet meal after a busy day in Theatre,' she told him in an attempt to lighten his mood. Sarah had been calm and forthright when she explained how she'd ended up in the emergency department in extreme abdominal pain after a heavy fall while out walking in Hagley Park. 'She told me she'd been referred to the public system but that she wanted to go private with the practice I work at.'

'Relax, Georgie. I'm more than happy that you're here, especially as a friend.' His smile was looking less strained by the minute. Then it wavered. 'Dad's not pleased to be presiding over the trial of those two men caught bringing in ten million dollars' worth of cocaine last year. It's going to run for four weeks. He'd far rather be here with Mum.'

'Bad timing.' High court judge Alistair Newman had spoken to Georgie earlier that morning to once again say thanks for supporting them. He was worried sick about his wife having to undergo major surgery. As were they all. Looking at Blake, Georgie was surprised to see approval beaming out at her from those charcoal eyes. The grey used to be light and sparkly. So far today, she'd only seen the colour of wet tar. Until now. Though nowhere near sparkling, they were lighter. Relieved even. 'I think we need to let Andrew get on with his job rather than listen to us yabbering.'

Andrew laughed. 'It's fine. I've got a

few minutes to spare. But…' He shrugged. 'Blake, come here.' He indicated the screen on the desk. 'Look at the MRI. It shows the clearest image of what's causing Sarah so much pain.'

Blake crossed over and stared at the images, the colour draining from his face. The fibroid pressing on Sarah's uterus was so big it made her stomach extend outward, which she'd put down to eating too many sweet delicacies lately.

Georgie heard Blake suck in air at the sight of the fibroid mass, saw his hands tighten, but he didn't say a word. Probably didn't want to scare his mum.

But Sarah was a GP and understood her problem, including the swelling on the walls of the uterus. That was the bigger of the concerns here; it was an indicator of cancer, though so far Andrew hadn't seen anything to back that up. He tapped the screen. 'That's why we're doing a full hysterectomy.'

Blake winced. 'At least six weeks taking it easy, Mum.'

Georgie couldn't take her eyes off him. He was very attractive now that she was seeing him as a man. Like blood-warming, stomach-tightening attractive. Gone were the laughter lines and cheeky twinkle in those eyes, sure, but there was a strength in his face, and a maturity that hadn't been there when she'd known him all those years ago. Interesting that she was even noticing. She didn't get overly involved with men these days. Not after her marriage failed. Tommy, her husband, reckoned she didn't try hard enough to love him, and after one too many arguments he'd packed up and left, breaking her heart and making her more cautious than ever. She'd wanted to have a family with him, but after losing her baby it was too much to bear on top of Noah's death so she'd said she couldn't try again. Love hurt bad when it went wrong. Tommy had been right in that she had been afraid to open her heart too much because of her fear of her love going wrong. It had taken a while for her to see that, which kind of suggested his accusations were bang on. Which didn't bode well for any other relationship she might find herself in, so she was staying clear of love.

On the screen the X-ray taken at the

emergency department two weeks ago when Sarah was admitted with severe abdominal pain appeared. 'This is what led to the scan showing the size of the fibroid and the other problem.' Andrew gave him a few minutes to take it in.

Blake nodded when he'd finished studying the image with an intensity that would've been scary if Georgie hadn't known he was thinking of his mother.

'We've done routine blood tests and everything's normal. A cross match has been done and bloods are on hold for tomorrow, in case a haemorrhage occurs, which isn't infrequent with this type of surgery. It helps Sarah's fit and otherwise healthy.' Andrew turned to Sarah. 'Anything else you would like to go over before tomorrow?'

'No, nothing. I just want it over with.'

Blake said to Andrew, 'I can't thank you enough for getting on to it so quickly.' Which implied he was even more worried than he'd shown so far, because there was nothing out of the ordinary about how soon the operation was being performed.

Andrew stood up and shook Blake's hand. 'No problem.'

Out in the corridor Blake's sombre eyes locked onto Georgie as though they were connected in all ways about this. Which, with the history of Noah there with them, they probably were.

Her stomach knotted. Touching his arm briefly, she said, 'We'll get through this.' Somehow she'd make sure of it. And she meant it when she'd said 'we.' They mightn't have stood by each other when Noah died because they'd both been struggling so much with their own grief to allow anyone else's in, but they had gone through the same pain and lived with the consequences in their own ways, and now could understand each other a little. Could understand the fear of losing Sarah.

'It's hard.' His voice was heavy.

'Yes.' He wouldn't have been expecting his mother to be undergoing surgery for a fibroid or possible cancer. No one ever did. She'd seen the shock in the faces of too many patients learning they had a serious problem so knew Blake was feeling it, if trying not to show his concerns. Turning away from that interesting but worried face, she drew a breath and calmly asked Sarah,

'You all right?' After the meeting with her surgeon about the procedure, it would feel more real than it had before. Very real.

'Pretty much as well as expected.' There was a waver in her voice.

'You can always ring me if you want to go over anything.'

And, Blake, try to stop worrying.

'I will.' Sarah gave her a hug. 'Thank you for being here. It makes everything easier somehow knowing you're looking out for me as a friend and doctor.'

Make me want to cry, why don't you?

This was why she didn't like getting close to people. Hadn't since Noah was taken from them. 'You couldn't keep me away.' She glanced at Blake and was surprised to see him nodding. He was happy she was here? When they'd not seen each other at all for so long? It did surprise her, though he used to try and get her attention when they were younger. When the boys finished high school and moved south to Dunedin and university where she was training to become a doctor she had caught up with them regularly. She'd been studying hard with a bit of partying on the side

whenever possible. Blake had been partying hard and cramming his studies in between. It's how it was for students in their
first couple of years before they settled into
serious study.

Then the night of the phone call came
and her world fell apart. Nothing was ever
to be the same again. She didn't know how
to grieve, how to move forward. Everyone
had advice, but they hadn't been there and
couldn't understand why she couldn't spend
six months crying, then pack up her feelings and get on with her life. In the end she
had done almost that, turned to study and
training as hard as she could, focusing on
her career and the goals she'd set before
she'd even left school. No more parties, no
more nights out with the girlfriends. But
the pain never left, downsized, maybe, but
it was always ready to roar to life whenever
something else went wrong.

That was the past, and her future had
been about being serious and careful so her
mum and dad could rely on her to be there
for them for ever. She'd even transferred
back to Christchurch to finish her training so they could see her whenever they

needed to, only leaving town for training stints in other hospitals up and down the country. Then she'd met Tommy and fallen in love and got married. Only she hadn't really given him her whole heart, had been afraid of being hurt again, and in the end *she'd* hurt Tommy, and herself as well.

'Sarah, I'll pop in to see you tomorrow morning in the pre-op room. You'll get to see me all glammed up in baggy scrubs.'

'Can't wait.' Sarah's face suddenly dropped.

Georgie reached for her hand. 'You'll be fine. We've got this.'

Don't break down. Not now.

Though if ever there was a moment for Sarah to fall apart it would be with Blake at her side. She adored her son even though he'd abandoned them for the most part. Until now when he was here to help and support his family.

'Come on, Mum, let's go home and wait for Dad to finish up for the day.' Blake gently took her arm to lead her away. Over his mother's head, he said, 'See you tomorrow?'

Georgie nodded. 'Of course. I'll drop by between surgeries.'

Bet Blake would be waiting when Sarah was wheeled into her room after recovery. He'd want to see for himself that she'd come through all right. More importantly, he'd want to hear what Andrew had to say about the surgery and what he'd found and if his mother had cancer or not. Until then, he wouldn't begin to relax. 'Catch you tomorrow.'

Watching him lead his mother out of the clinic, she drew a long, shaky breath. Strange how she was really looking forward to seeing him again, and it had nothing to do with talking about Sarah's condition. She'd never once thought of Blake Newman as anything but Noah's mate. Who'd have believed he'd grow up so damned good-looking?

There had been a drought of men lately but surely that had nothing to do with her reacting to Blake like he was necessary to her. She didn't have it in her to get deeply involved with men any more, or anyone, really. The few men she'd dated lately seemed to want the whole caboodle, almost before they took the time to get to know her very well. She didn't want to take another chance on finding happiness. She'd blown it twice before so didn't believe she'd be that lucky. The relationship she'd been in when Noah died had collapsed because she couldn't function properly, and then her marriage, which for all its faults could've been good if only she'd known how to let go the strings tying down her heart. She and Tommy would've doted on their child, if only—

'If only' was a mantra from her past.

There were barriers to lower before any relationship was likely to happen. Barriers that were now so ensconced in her makeup it would take a bulldozer to move them. Anyway, it was preferable to protect her heart, and concentrate on her career.

Georgie's eyes followed Blake's tall figure walking at a slow pace matching his mother's weary one, his head on an angle as he listened to her. Now that she'd caught up with him Georgie felt he might be a man she'd always be aware of, if he was in town, which he hardly ever was.

Really? Why did she think that? She didn't usually just see a guy and go, 'He's the one for me.' Not that she'd had that decimating thought today, but there were tweaks going on in her body that spoke of interest and long-forgotten excitement over spending time with a virile man. 'Blake,' she called and headed after him. 'Blake, hold on a minute.' Why was she doing this? If he needed to contact her he'd find a way.

'Yes, Georgie?'

She shivered. Her name sounded different coming off his tongue. Softer. Sexier? How likely was that? She hadn't noticed she was getting desperate for a man, but perhaps that's what these unexplainable sensations he invoked were all about. Nah, hardly. This was all about Blake, and nothing, nobody, else.

'Georgie?' Now he sounded concerned. Next he'd be thinking she knew something he didn't about his mother.

'If you need to get in touch at any time, Sarah's got my private number.'

Sarah turned, a soft smile lighting up her eyes. 'I gave it to him already.'

Air whooshed out of her lungs. 'Right. Okay. That's fine.' Not that she expected Blake to be ringing to ask her about the operation. He'd get the details from Andrew.

So was she expecting him to phone for the hell of it? To have a chat about the weather? Georgie swallowed the disappointment the idea of not hearing from him brought on. It wasn't as though she had any reason to expect him to be in touch. They were all but strangers after all, even though there was a sense of togetherness about Sarah and her op tripping through her at the moment. 'See you tomorrow.' Sometime. Maybe. If he was around when she dropped by. She turned back towards her office.

'Georgie, thank you for looking out for Mum. It's made it easier for her, having another medical mind to download with. I know Dad feels the same.'

Pausing, she stared up at Blake, who'd returned to stand close to her. For once she was seeing him as the guy she used to know, seeing his gentleness in battle with his determination to always be the best at everything. They'd got on as much as two young people with their age difference could. Noah had been their common denominator whenever they were in the same space, but they'd never been best friends or anywhere close. She'd felt grown up while thinking he had a way to go on that score. Regret filled her. What if they had known each other better? Would they have been able to help one another through the tragedy that struck? Would a friendship have softened the pain any? Probably not. Anyway, it hadn't been and nothing could change how they'd both managed to carry on with their individual lives. 'So has you being here for Sarah. She was thrilled when you told her you were coming home for this week.'

'Fortnight.' He seemed surprised he'd said that, as if he'd just had the thought. 'Talk later.' He turned to go back to his mother's side.

Georgie watched him walking purposefully, head high, back straight. The new, grown-up, empathetic Blake she'd never met before. The tip of her tongue touched the centre of her top lip. Fifteen minutes and already she liked him as much as the younger, cheeky version. Oh, those dark curls. They were begging to have her fingers run through them. But most of all, her heart wanted to soften his worry, take away the fear that was spilling out of his eyes whenever he looked at Sarah.

She'd be there if Blake should want to talk.

Hands behind his head, Blake lay on the bed in what had been his room since he was a toddler, and stared at the rafters. A vision of a certain gynaecologist startled him, teasing him with its clarity.

Georgie had matured into an absolutely stunning woman.

And that wasn't the half of what was stirring him up. Her confidence and calmness was new. To him any rate. Okay, maybe she'd always been confident in a do-as-I-say kind of way. But calm? Not even close. A hurricane on legs. And what legs they were. Still were from what he'd seen highlighted by a fitted black skirt that barely reached her knees. That had been Georgie when they were growing up in the suburb of Fendalton. A hurricane that puttered out to a breeze when Noah died. Not that he'd seen her since the funeral and she hadn't been aware of him that day. He'd sat squeezed between his father and mother, and deliberately refrained from talking to her for fear of increasing the pain she was suffering. The kind of fear that had lived with him ever since the night Noah died, fear that dominated how he approached everything, especially getting close to others, of hurting others. Yes, he was a bit of loner nowadays. A bit? Mostly a lone wolf, more like. He had friends, didn't he? Friends he did his best not to get too close to, though their offspring did make a mockery of that at times with their straightforward approach, the little ratbags.

He sighed. Georgie and those legs brought back other memories. In the past he'd seen them coming out of short shorts, from below tennis skirts that stretched across her thighs accentuating the muscles and curves and eating up the pavement when she went for a run. Georgie was Noah's older sister, not overly interested in what he and her brother were up to, though always there for advice when they moved to Dunedin to attend university. She was always on the go, studying, working, partying. Full of life. But yeah, as a horny eighteen-year-old he'd noticed Georgie far too much. And when he was nineteen. Then Noah was gone and so was the desire to get close to anyone.

Maybe Georgie was even more confident now. She had locked those stunning eyes on him whenever he spoke, tough as ever, but seeming bruised and a little withdrawn. She'd still take no prisoners, yet he felt that beneath the don't-mess-with-me exterior there was a woman who longed to be held, hugged, to be reassured she was still Georgie Price: daughter, sister, even a friend. He'd been told by his parents she was almost completely focused on her career now, especially since her marriage fell apart. Another blow to an already broken heart.

Feelings he understood too damned much. Nearly thirteen years since his life was abruptly flipped onto its back. Years of guilt and doubt, of starting over when it came to believing in himself, except he hadn't quite managed that yet. Sure, he'd done brilliantly in his training to become an orthopaedic surgeon and was now working in a private practice in Auckland. He had the perfect career, a small but reliable set of friends whom he kept at arm's length and an awesome family he did his best to keep away from because they got under his shield and into his heart far too easily. But he did miss love, the belonging, the cohesiveness of being a part of a loving environment. It was lonely at night when he was finished with work or socialising and headed home to his beautiful but empty house, the cold sheets on his bed, a glass of wine on the deck with no one to grump about his day with. Was he feeling sorry for himself? Good point. It was time to get over himself and look beyond his own fears. If he knew how, or had the courage to give it a go.

His mother was ill. How ill, no one would know until after tomorrow's operation, and even then, there would be no surety in the answer about cancer until the lab report come back. Andrew had hesitated when he said he was fairly certain Mum didn't have cancer, but that was doctor-speak for not laying it on the line without proof. His mum said Georgie doubted cancer was in the uterus after she'd seen the scan and MRI, and a part of him believed her. Perhaps that was him wanting her to be right. But he was a son fearing the worst and afraid to accept Georgie's conclusion in case that tempted the opposite result. Funny though how much he wanted to trust her verdict, even when she could only say she was ninety per cent sure his mother didn't have cancer. He shivered. He just had to get through the night and half the morning and there'd be some answers. Fingers crossed.

Georgie was stirring him in strange ways. Not that she'd said anything out of the ordinary to start him wondering about how he felt about her. The past hadn't been mentioned. Why would it be? Especially in the hospital when the focus was on his mother. But make no mistake, there was something between them. A hint of wonder, of belief, between them. Or had he felt it more because she'd been both professional and friendly without being too much of either, and therefore these emotions were running rampant? Because she was his mirror image when it came to the past and how they'd coped? He'd shut down on his heart, afraid to take any chance on being so badly hurt again. It made perfect sense Georgie might've done the same.

What was she doing right now? Relaxing before her surgery schedule tomorrow? Uptight about his mother's operation? Everyone seemed to be on the same page over that. His mother was stressing to bits while pretending all was fine and that she'd get through this like a piece of cake. Dad wasn't much better, saying little about what they were dealing with, preferring to chat about the case he was judging without actually telling him anything.

Georgie and Andrew may have said there was a remote chance that cancer was causing the swelling in the uterus wall, but he knew from personal experience with patients that once the C word was out there no one relaxed until the pathology came through saying negative. Pathology took days, if not weeks, to read samples and make a diagnosis.

Damn this. He was getting too despondent when there was nothing he could do but wait until tomorrow for any answers to the questions battering his mind. Getting off the bed, Blake crossed to the window to look down on the familiar street. The streetlights had come on as the sun made its last hurrah on the edge of the city. As a teen those lights used to annoy him when he was trying to sneak out the window to go join his mates at the park at the end of the road for an hour of talking nonsense and listening to hip-hop on someone's phone. They used to think that was the best in music. Nowadays he'd turn it off if it came on anywhere near his ears.

Georgie and her girlfriends would dance to it, shaking and bobbing around like they'd lost control of themselves on the lawn or the deck. Probably had, when he thought about the half-empty bottle of vodka he and Noah found behind her father's rosebushes one evening after the girls had gone to a nightclub in town.

Georgie didn't look like a woman who partied any more. Had she lost the zest for life that had been her trademark when she lost Noah? At first he'd gone the other way, taking up drinking and partying in a big way, stopped studying so hard as he tried to fill the gap Noah had left in an attempt to prove he was okay. But the feeling that a piece of him was missing and would never come back hadn't left him. He'd struggled to stifle the guilt for not being there to talk his mate out of taking a ride with a drunk that night. If not for Noah's father telling him to let it all go and stop ruining his own life who knew where he might've ended up? It didn't bear thinking about. A deep longing to talk to someone who knew him from the past filled him. It would be wonderful to talk without having to consider the other person wouldn't have a clue what he was on about. Someone who'd understand why he was so worried about his mother.

'What if Mum's got cancer?' he asked for the thousandth time. All very well saying they'd deal with it, that she'd be all right, but cancer had a mind of its own, and tough as his mum was, she might not win that particular battle. She'd certainly give it everything she had, and some, but cancer was a devil. He could not lose his mother. Neither could his sisters, or their children lose their grandmother. As for dad, he'd be decimated. He was already struggling with waiting for tomorrow to be over and them to have some idea where they were headed. Blake shuddered. If his dad was in a bad way, then so was he because he'd never let anyone come near him even to share a meal, let alone know his heart, if the worst happened. Losing Noah had been devastating, and call him naïve, or whatever word came to mind, but he didn't want to face that again. Yet life did throw curve balls. It was how it was. Just not tomorrow or his mum or his family.

Please.

Blake watched a young couple strolling along the footpath, holding hands as they chattered. His heart crunched for what might've been if life hadn't changed so abruptly the night Noah was in that accident. Love, laughter, children. Sure, his life wasn't exactly a desert. But love *was* missing. Someone to share his soul with. A woman to talk to, lie next to, make love with. Children were a dim dream. All because he couldn't let go of the past and look forward with hope and a smile.

Yet right this moment he wanted to share some of his fear and pain. Turning, he reached for his phone, picked it up and stared at the screen until the light went off. 'Nah, she'll think I'm crazy.' She might be

right too. He didn't do reaching out to anybody, let alone Georgie.

'Enough.' His head was a mess which
would keep him awake all night if he didn't
do something about it. Going for a run usually did the trick. He dug in his bag for his
gear.

Georgie ran along the riverbank, refusing to
think about anything or anyone. Like that
was working. Impossible. Blake kept coming to mind. How good he looked. How
worried he was over Sarah. How his tired
smile had hit her hard, and made her want
to be there for him no matter what.

A man ran past, turned around and ran
backwards slowly. 'Georgie.'

Could it be? 'Hello, Blake.' She slowed
to a brisk walk. Hard to talk while running.

He stepped in beside her. 'Small world,
eh?'

'Seems like it.' Of all the thousands of
people in the city it was Blake who ran by.

'You do this regularly?'

'Most days in summer when it's not dark
by the time I get home.' She'd been longing to talk to Blake all afternoon and here

he was. So talk. 'It's my way of destressing from the day so I can sleep at night. You're the same?'

'Yes, I am. Of course today's different. I seem to have been sitting around one place or another most of the day, and figured some exercise might quieten the brain.' He glanced her way. 'Do you still stay up all hours and rush into work late?' There was light laughter in his voice that made her all warm and cosy.

'I try to be a bit more sensible these days.' She was so damned sensible it was boring even for her. She might be thirty-six but that didn't mean she had to start behaving like her grandmother. Actually, that was unfair on Gran. Gran was never at home, always out with her friends or walking in the hills around Diamond Harbour or helping at one of the community shops in town.

'Never thought I'd hear you say something like that.' Then his voice went flat. 'It's been a long time, hasn't it?'

Not going there. Seeing the worry in Blake's face earlier in the day had brought back her own past pain which she didn't need right now. 'Sarah's filled me in on some of the things you've been doing, including taking up a partnership in an orthopaedic clinic in central Auckland a couple of months ago. That's awesome.'

'You're a partner at Scott's Women's Health. Equally awesome. The pair of us have done all right. Career-wise any rate.'

'I used my training as an escape from joining in everything else going on around me.' A sigh escaped. Talking about this was unusual for her. Was it the same for Blake? But she wasn't ready to stop. There was something cathartic about it she hadn't known before. 'Why did you choose orthopaedics?'

'Hard to say, other than when a team mate in the school rugby team broke his leg during a game I sort of pictured myself in Theatre helping him. I know, I'm weird, but it worked. These days I get immense satisfaction from getting people back on their feet, seeing their shock and relief when they realise they no longer have to put up with debilitating pain from an arthritic knee or hip, or can get back on their cycle once their shoulder is healed.' His voice resonated with enthusiasm and he walked easier. The conversation was on safe ground? 'What about you? Why gynaecology?'

'It was always my goal from the first day at med school. No idea why other than I've always been fascinated with the reproductive system and helping women with their problems gives me a sense of achievement I don't get with anything else.' She laughed. 'Like you, I love seeing patients realise they can move forward without pain or have the baby they'd once thought impossible.' Her laughter faded. 'Though I can't help everyone.'

'No one can, Georgie. No one.'

'How true.' Time to change the subject before she became maudlin. 'What else do you do with your time apart from work? Still hit a cricket ball around the paddock?'

'I've been known to on the rare occasions I go to watch one of my mates' sons play for his school. Have to say I'm useless nowadays. Don't seem to have the eye-hand-ball co-ordination I once had. I still run, go out fishing occasionally, and nowadays I take to the hills hiking a lot.'

'On your own?'

'Mostly.' Another pause, then, 'Because

it's less demanding, if you know what I mean?'

No one to get close to or find himself actually talking with about personal subjects. 'I'm afraid I do. Letting go the past hasn't been easy, and talking about it even harder. I've still a way to go, if I'm truthful.' And why wouldn't she be? Blake made her feel as though a weight was being lifted off her shoulders. 'Does that mean you haven't got a partner at the moment?' There hadn't been anyone to support him today when he'd been with his mother. That he needed someone there had been obvious by the tension in his shoulders as he'd paced the room. Georgie knew she'd try her best to be there for him over the coming days despite this strange new awareness of Blake that she'd been trying hard to ignore because that was way better than letting her suddenly over-reactive body get out of hand.

'Nope. First I was too busy studying and working to have time for anyone else, then—I don't know. Too much time spent working, I guess.'

'Sounds familiar. Though I was married for a while. It didn't work out.'

'Did you marry that guy you met at university? If I remember rightly, you moved in with him in my second year.'

'Spenser. No, we didn't last long after Noah died. I was too wrapped up in my grief and he couldn't handle it. I wasn't a lot of fun any more.'

'You were better off without him if that's the way he treated you.'

He certainly knew how to make her feel all warm and soft. 'Thanks, but I wasn't easy to be around at the time.'

Blake looked her way. 'So? That's no excuse. He was your partner. He was supposed to support you.'

You would. Deep inside she believed that. He'd blamed himself for not being with Noah, who was so upset about being dumped by his girlfriend that he got drunk and then got in a car driven by a guy who was well over the limit. Blake had never let that happen again on his watch. 'Anyway, that's history. I'm flying solo these days. I have a couple of close friends I spend time with whenever possible, and it's enough.' Really? It had been. Why doubt it now? Her eyes slid sideways. Not because Blake

Newman had turned up in her day and made her blood hum. That was not reason enough to change anything.

'I know what that's like. I don't spend a lot of time with my mates and their families.'

Sounded like he tried to stay away from them more often than not. But then he would, having lost his best friend. 'I understand. I meant it when I said I'm available if you want to talk about Sarah. Or anything else.'

'Thanks. I appreciate that. A lot.' He stared ahead for a moment. Then, 'You've stayed in Christchurch all along?'

Ever since she came back after Noah died? 'Yes.' A part of her wanted to talk to him as she once might have, lighthearted and free, but she was held back by the constraints she'd put in place nearly thirteen years ago. She'd already said more than normal. Seeing Blake's distress over Sarah had brought back the past with a bang, and her stomach churning with the need to share things with him, but how did one start saying stuff that had been kept under wraps for so long? Things that had probably hurt them both. Did he wonder what Noah might have been like nowadays? If he'd set up the architectural business he was passionate about? Married and had kids?

Let loose a bit, speak from your heart, not the left side of your brain.

Deep breath. Could she let Blake in where she allowed no one? But then Blake was a part of the past that had closed down her happy spirit and brought her back to Christchurch permanently. She understood all too well why he was so worried. 'At first I came back to be here for Mum and Dad. Then I realised it worked for me too. I wanted to be close to them for my own sake.' Her mouth dried. She hadn't put any of this into words in a long time, if at all. She'd tried not to dump her sadness on Tommy, and in hindsight, that was probably unfair since he did cop her mood swings, and because he'd wanted to know all of her, not only selective pieces of her past.

Blake was quiet, yet she didn't feel uncomfortable, more as though he was giving her time and space to carry on if she chose to.

So she did. 'In some ways it was hard.

They kept checking up on me, like they were afraid I'd vanish off the planet one day. But then I pretty much did the same with them. It became our norm for a long time.' Over the years they'd all relaxed a little, but not completely.

'That's natural after what happened.'

'I guess. These days we're back to some semblance of what used to be our family normal, but I can't drop the fact that I should be here so that they're able to see me whenever they want. Not that I'm complaining. Christchurch is my hometown. I work in a private practice as well as at the public hospital. Most of my friends are still here. What more could I want?' Now she'd said it, she realised she was happy. Maybe in a quieter, less full-on way than she was when she was young, but happy none the less. Some of her dreams hadn't been fulfilled, but no one got everything they wanted. 'Honestly, I like living here. It's where I grew up, and I'm comfortable.'

See what talking from the heart did? It showed her she wasn't really deeply involved in anything other than work. A career she was very proud of. Her achievements made her feel good. In a lonely kind of way, really. Comfortable wasn't exactly exciting. So what about the biggest dream of them all? A man to love. Throw children in the mix and she'd be ecstatic. Except she'd lost a baby once, and didn't think she could face that if it were to happen again.

Drop it, Georgie. Talk with Blake while you've got the opportunity.

'What about you? Are you happy in Auckland? Got a good life going up there?'

Blake shrugged. 'I have my own home and the career I want. It's enough.'

Didn't sound like it by a long shot. They walked in silence for a few minutes.

Blake appeared to be miles away until he asked, 'Didn't your parents buy a camper-van a little while ago?'

'You're not entirely out of touch then. Yes, they bought one of those big suckers and have managed to get away for short trips a few times lately when they're not bogged down with their jobs. In fact right now they're away for a couple of weeks on the West Coast. I know they want to do the North Island sometime. As in take months, stopping for long periods in places that interest them, moving on wherever the urge takes them.'

'I have called in to see them on a few of the occasions I've been back to see Mum and Dad. They were always good to me as a teenager. And later…' Blake's voice trailed off.

'I know they love hearing from you.'

And now she might be understanding a little better why, because deep inside there was a sensation of tension easing that she hadn't known she was carrying. Almost as if one small piece of her had clicked into place. The start of a zip closing, one tooth shut, many more to go. Something to look forward to? Yes, it might be. All because she'd caught up with Blake and was talking with him like there was nothing to feel uncomfortable about. As if she'd found the one thing that had been missing in her life for so long. Defining what that was might take a while, but one click showed it was possible. Whatever *it* was. Georgie stopped walking. 'That's my car. Do you want a lift home?'

'No, I'm good.' He was looking directly at her. 'It's been good catching up.'

'I agree.' Unexpected as it was, talking with Blake had reminded her of the past without the pain. Of course she still hurt, but Blake had been there, understood more than any of her friends what it was like to lose Noah. 'I'll see you tomorrow.'

'Will do.' He was gone. Hopefully only for a few hours, not years.

He'd be at the hospital with Sarah tomorrow, and possibly the day after and maybe the next one too, so she would see him some more. Where had this need to get to know Blake come from? It was new, for sure. And worrying. No, make that intriguing. It made her body heat and her skin soften. And her fears loosen a teeny-weeny bit. Sensations she hadn't known in for ever. Bring them on.

Surely not? Surely yes. She headed for home, feeling more enthusiastic about everything than she had in a long, long time.

CHAPTER TWO

'YOU'LL BE FINE, Mum.' Blake kissed his mother's forehead gently. *You'd better be.* 'I'll be waiting for you when you're taken back to your room.' *Hopefully your surgeon will be right behind you.*

He needed to hear that his mother was in the clear and only had the operation to recover from. Not that it was a minor op, but way better than the alternative.

And hopefully Georgie would turn up at some stage. He couldn't wait to see her again, which was kind of bizarre considering they hadn't meant anything to each other before. *We don't now.* Yeah, but he sensed he wanted to. They had something in common—they'd cut themselves off from normal lives because of the past. Georgie hadn't come out and said as much but it was there in her empathy and support yesterday. Also in her voice when they'd talked last night. She made him feel less alone. No one had made him feel that way in so long an ache was beating in his head.

During the long, sleepless hours—running and walking hadn't helped—the idea of spending some time with her had kept circling around his worry over his mother. It was as though Georgie had thrown him a lifeline that he couldn't quite catch. Let her in, or keep pushing her away as per normal? Sink or swim? For the first time in for ever the idea of letting go some of the fear holding him down was tempting. But not tempting enough to actually follow through. Though getting a little closer to Georgie was also tempting, with nothing to lose if it didn't work out. He'd be gone within a couple of weeks, back to reality.

Beside him his mother murmured, 'I know I will.' Except she wasn't looking so confident now that the pre-op room was just through the door and a nurse was taking her BP. 'I'm a doctor. I understand what's happening.'

Understanding was one thing. Being afraid

was quite another. In this case one probably led to the other because of her medical knowledge as a GP. She knew all too well how badly this could end up. Blake held his breath, willing the sudden blockage in his throat to dissolve so he could talk properly without giving away his emotions and adding to her worries.

His dad held his mother's hand, squeezing gently. 'I imagine it's different when you're the patient, darling. Just remember you're a fighter.'

Blake looked from one parent to the other, saw the look of understanding passing between them. His parents had always been strong and fought for their children and raised them to be equally tough. What was always apparent was the love these two had for each other. After thirty-three years together—married in haste because he was on the way, unplanned for but looked forward to—and they still adored each other as though they'd just fallen in love. They'd added two daughters to the mix. Despite staying out of their lives, he loved his sisters, both of whom were married and lived in rural Canterbury. They'd said they'd be dropping in to see their mother after her operation. They were busy with their kids, and their families' businesses, and were thrilled when he said he'd come down to be around to help when Mum went home. Home. Families. Partners.

A shiver rocked him as a wave of longing rolled through his tense body. What he wouldn't give to have the same. Someone to love and trust implicitly, to share the good and not so good with, to raise children with, to age and climb into their rocking chairs side by side and cuddle grandchildren alongside each other. Except he was lying to himself. He was not prepared to chance his heart again. That he was already afraid of what was happening with his mother.

'Morning, Sarah.' The voice that had followed him into bed and finally a brief sleep cut through his wandering mind. Talking with her had started him relaxing a little and then he'd begun wondering if he should also try to get home to see his family more often. It was as if Georgie had made him aware of how he'd been missing out on being with them, if only to talk and laugh together.

'Hello, Georgie,' his mother said. 'It's lovely of you to drop by. I know you're busy.'

Georgie winked. 'You haven't seen me. I can't stay, but wanted to say hello to you all.' She turned and smiled at him. 'Morning.'

A smile Blake felt deep inside. 'You're looking perky.' Like old times when she never seemed to stop smiling or laughing.

Then her smile slipped a little, suggesting it was a brave face for his parents, and maybe for him. Then it came back, bigger and brighter. Yeah, definitely a brave face. 'Of course I am. A good night's sleep is all it takes.'

Wish he could say the same. Talking to Georgie last night had added to the list of things to overthink and worry about. At the same time he'd come to realise he was glad he'd returned to be with his family through this distressing time. Catching up with this woman was a bonus he hadn't expected. 'I think you've cheered up Mum a little.' And him. There was definitely a lightness in his veins he hadn't expected. Could be he was being cheered up the most here.

Georgie kissed his mother on the forehead. 'Good luck. See you later.'

Oh, hell. Reality check.

Please be all right, Mum. Come through the surgery and not have cancer. Please.

Gulp. Hell, any minute now he was going to embarrass himself with tears spilling down his cheeks if he wasn't careful.

Georgie nodded at him with a gentle smile on her lovely mouth—as though she knew exactly what was going on inside his head.

Face it. She probably did, being a doctor and used to seeing pain in the faces of patients' loved ones. 'Bye,' was all he could manage.

'Right, Theatre waits for no one.' She was gone, a whirlwind of energy and focus. Surgeon on a mission. Friend supporting friends. Georgie of old in a new camouflage.

The pre-op nurse bustled in and went to the end of the bed to undo the wheel brakes with her foot. 'Let's do this, Sarah.'

Blake closed his eyes for a moment.

This is it. In a few hours we will have

some answers, will know if Mum's safe, or if there's more stress and grief to come.

Hell, he'd believed he understood what his patients' loved ones went through when they were going into Theatre. He hadn't had a clue. There should be a paper about this that all doctors had to sit before they qualified to make them fully aware of the anguish people faced. It was a very lonely time, even with his dad here. But he did have Georgie onside. Even when she wasn't right here physically, she understood his torment.

Blake's father kissed his wife, locking his eyes with hers for a long moment, sending messages in their silent love language. Then he straightened, said, 'Be safe, sweetheart,' and turned away, surreptitiously brushing the back of his hand over his face.

Leaning over the bed, Blake gave his mum another peck on the cheek. 'See you soon.' Then he watched the nurse wheel her out of the room and down the hall towards Theatre, his heart heavy and his brain filled with worry. 'Come on, Dad. We'll go over the road and grab a coffee and some breakfast before you head to court.' He needed the distraction, and so did his dad.

'Yeah.' The older man's voice was clogged with tears. 'Yeah.' For the first time that Blake could recall he really did sound old. Or was that because he hadn't been around enough to notice his father aging? Something else to think about. There were a few hits coming his way at the moment. He straightened a little. He'd take them, and hopefully learn something along the way to improve his outlook on the future.

'She'll be fine.' Draping an arm over his dad's shoulders, Blake led him outside. 'She's got you, Dad. That's more important.'

'Georgie gives me confidence even when I know this operation isn't in her hands,' Dad said.

Blake agreed. 'There's something about her that makes me want to believe everything will be fine, that she won't countenance anything going wrong for Mum even when she won't be there. It's nothing new. She always exuded a confidence that was hard not to accept.' Only it used to come with laughter and jokes and fun. There'd been a seriousness behind all that, but she was great to be around. Not that he and Noah had spent a lot of time in her space because she hadn't wanted them hanging around, but he did remember how warm and happy she made him feel when sharing the same air. Could he feel that again?

'She's never faltered in her determination to be the best at what she does. And that's not only in her profession,' his dad added.

What else was going on in Georgie's life? Not a question to put to his father. If he wanted to know, he'd ask Georgie outright. Yes, he'd do just that. Even if it was only to get to know more about her. It might help him let go the past. Some of it anyway. Right then he decided that he was going to see some more of her, starting with inviting her out to dinner tonight. He only planned on spending a week in Christchurch so he needed to make good use of his time. Of course there was the following week when he'd intended doing some overdue work around his house, maybe even taking the boat for a jaunt on the Waitemata looking for fish. Hadn't he inadvertently said to Georgie he was here for two weeks? See?

She'd got to him that early on, tossing common sense out the door like a piece of garbage. Though it wasn't hard when his focus had been almost entirely on his mother. Yet strange how spending a week in Auckland paled into insignificance when he considered the possibility of staying on to spend more time with his family and maybe get to know Georgie as he hadn't before. Because she did understand what he was going through at the moment? Or was there more to this new interest? Hopefully she'd join him for a meal or two, maybe take a day trip out to Akaroa. As long as his mother was doing well after her surgery. Going further than a few minutes' drive away wasn't happening otherwise.

Time to stop overthinking everything. 'Want to talk about the trial, Dad?' There wouldn't be a lot he could say but from past experience Blake knew he liked to vent when a trial went on for too long and there was a lot of repetition in the questions put to witnesses.

'It's doing my head in. You'd think by now I'd understand why people went off the rails, but I'm darned if I do.'

This was the man who'd told Noah's dad how afraid he was that Blake was wrecking his chances of a wonderful career and future. Even now Blake felt the relief at having listened to Lucas, who'd taken on board what his dad had said and immediately hopped on a plane to Dunedin to talk to him. Lucas had turned him around before he made a complete mess of everything by making him understand how his waywardness wasn't solving anything, instead adding to everyone's stress. Blake had been grateful ever since. He owed Lucas, and his father. 'You do fine, Dad.'

In the café, with coffees and bacon and eggs before them, they continued talking about anything and everything except Blake's mother's operation and the trial his dad was ruling over. At eight on the dot, his father pushed his plate and mug aside, and stood up. 'I'll see you tonight. Keep me up to date on everything.' Then he was striding away, leaving Blake feeling bereft of his company.

Odd because he hardly ever spent time with him. But today there was a bubble of anticipation rising within him, and he wanted to share it, examine it with someone who'd not laugh at him. Georgie came to mind. Except he'd deliberately avoided mentioning her. Oh, yes, that would've worked a treat when his father had a soft spot for her and liked to bring her into conversations far too often.

Hey, Georgie, you're pressing all my buttons in ways I've never known and I want to talk to you about that.

For the record, she was the last person he'd talk to about these new sensations.

She'd laugh her beautiful head off. Tell him to get a life, as she used to often enough when he and Noah were trying to join her and her girlfriends for some fun. Actually, he'd enjoy hearing her laugh. She looked as if she needed to let off steam occasionally, as though the last few years had been all hard work and not a lot of fun. Which sounded a little too familiar.

'Can I get you anything else?'

He looked up at the waitress clearing the plates from the table. 'No, I'm good, thanks.' Yeah, and what was he going to do next? Wander along the bank of the Avon? That wasn't such a bad idea. He could do that—later. 'Actually, I'll have another long black, please.' It wasn't as though he didn't have plenty of time on hand.

Andrew had said the op would likely take up to two and a half hours, which meant if he'd started on time he wouldn't be finished until ten at the absolute earliest. Then his mother would be in recovery for a while so no visiting going on. Or any discussion about what the op had revealed. Coffee was a good choice right now, filling in a few minutes at least.

Blake took his time over the coffee, reading news headlines on his phone in-between watching people coming in for coffee or food on their way to work. Next he tried to stroll along the riverbank, but strolling wasn't really his style, so he changed direction and headed over the bridge and in the direction of his old school. As he approached he saw boys dressed smartly in uniform standing in huddles by the gate and further inside the fenced grounds where the imposing stone buildings dominated the landscape, talking and laughing as only teens could.

Memories stirred. He and Noah laughing uproariously over their mate's attempt to leap the fence when it was higher than he was tall. Complaining about the little time they had to play rugby. Plotting how to get girls to notice them. Yeah, those had been fun times. They'd also worked hard and totally believed they could be whoever they wanted, and thought university would be a walk in the park. They took driving lessons at the same time, played in the same sports teams on those fields behind the impressive stone building facing the street and fought to get higher grades than the other. Competitive yet loyal, egging each other on into trouble while always having one another's back. That friendship had started at these very gates on the first day of term of year nine when he accidently slammed into Noah in his haste to get to the office. He'd never forget the cheeky grin that met him as Noah staggered back onto his feet, pointed at him and said, 'You'll pay for that, pal.'

'You think? Pal.' He'd smirked, like any hormonal just-becoming-a-teenager lad was prone to do.

'You any good at boxing?'

'I can go ten rounds,' he'd lied. Then

laughed because he liked the look of the guy. 'Kidding. I'd be rubbish. But I know how to bowl a cricket ball.' He'd seen the red ball in a side pocket of the guy's backpack.

'Cool. Let's go toss a few pitches.' From then on they'd become inseparable. As easy as that.

Blake stood, hands in his pockets as a couple of cars pulled in and more boys leapt out and hurried through the gates. The best days of his life had been behind that fence. 'Damn it, Noah. We sure knew how to have a blast. Miss you, mate.' So much his life had stalled when Noah left them, and had never returned to full speed again. Some parts hadn't moved at all. Love being the biggest one. He swallowed hard. Looking around at the buildings, the immaculate grounds, the boys, some awkward, others overly confident as they strode across to the assembly hall, he felt something loosening inside him. They'd believed they held life in their hands, and that it'd only get better. Now he knew different. But had he wasted what he'd been given? Would Noah be proud of him for shutting down like he had? For walking away from everything and everyone he loved? Absolutely not, was the honest answer. And he owed Noah and himself that much at least.

A shiver lifted the skin on Blake's arms. What had he done? Thrown everything to the wind? Given up too easily? Yes, Noah would be furious with him for dropping the ball. For not being around for his family. For not letting them help him when he grieved so deeply. Georgie said returning home had been good for her. It would've been the same for him too. Was it too late to change so he could have love and affection, and share himself with his parents and sisters and their families? To have a woman to love, and maybe even children?

Damn it, Blake. Stop this.

Turning away, he strode purposefully toward the private hospital. He was in Christchurch to support his family, and not to up-end his own world. Not to start thinking there was more to Georgie than a friend from the past. Not to let Noah trip him up.

He arrived back at the hospital just after ten thirty to be told his mother wasn't out of surgery. Was that good or bad? Or routine? Due to a later start than scheduled?

'Now what?' he said without thinking.

'You're a friend of Georgie's, aren't you?' a nurse walking past asked.

'Yes.' How did the nurse know that? Friend was one word for whatever they had going. Try a shadow from her past who'd like to get to know her way better than as his best friend's sister. Though he'd decided that he wasn't going there. But it was impossible to ignore the need to get a little closer to her. Friend would be great, really. A true, close friend he could talk to about anything, including the guilt he still carried about Noah when knowing he didn't need to.

'Georgie mentioned Mrs Newman's son was here. You're a doctor, aren't you?' the guy asked.

'Orthopaedic surgeon.' He tried to keep the pride from spilling over but by the look of amusement on the nurse's face he knew he hadn't got away with it. 'Just another arrogant specialist who thinks the rest of you owe me something for even putting my scrubs on,' he muttered.

And got laughed at in return. 'I've dealt with my share of those. But you are not talking about Georgie when you say that. She's mindful of everyone who works here. She could be full of herself because she is a brilliant doctor but she acts as one cog in a whole wheel of them.'

'You're not telling me anything I don't know.' Or hadn't guessed. 'Obviously I haven't worked with her as our fields are very different, and I didn't start training until she had nearly finished, but that sounds like the Georgie I knew.' He shouldn't be talking to this guy about her, but he couldn't stop thinking about her and wanting to hear her name on his tongue. But. Okay. Shut up. 'I'd better go find something to do while I wait for my mother to come out of Theatre.'

Heading into the city, he passed a florist, and backtracked to go inside.

'Can I help you?' the woman behind the counter tying a bundle of roses together with a bright red ribbon asked.

'Have you got any sweet peas?' His mum's favourite.

'There are some out the back. Would you

like me to put a bunch together or make a bouquet with an assortment of other flowers?'

'A big bunch of only sweet peas would be perfect.' No-fuss Mum would prefer that over a fancy bouquet any day. 'I'll take those roses too, unless they're for an order.' Georgie came to mind for those. Bright, colourful and full of life. The old Georgie who had started to peek through the shutters on the two occasions he talked with her or watched her with his mother.

'They're yours.'

Pulling into the hospital carpark he drew a wobbly breath. What was he doing, buying flowers for Georgie? She'd think he'd lost his mind. It was less than twenty-four hours since he'd first seen her after so long and he'd bought her flowers. Anyone would think he was wooing her, and that so wasn't the case. He was interested in getting to know her as adults, but that's where it had to stop. He was settled in Auckland with the perfect job and ideal home for a single man. Georgie lived here, in the South Island, obviously happy with her work and having family and friends nearby. Damn it. He left the roses on the seat when he got out of the car, and slammed the door shut on his frustration. Should never have left Auckland.

Instantly remorse rose. 'Sorry, Mum.' As if he'd have stayed away while this was happening.

His phone beeped. Georgie.

'Heard anything?' she asked.

'Not a word.' He glanced at his watch. 'Should be any minute now.' He wasn't saying overdue, but the time it was taking to hear from the surgeon was winding him tighter than a ball of string.

'I'm between patients. Talk again soon.' She was gone.

Leaving Blake shaken. As though something was wrong and he didn't know what. But Georgie had nothing to do with his mother's surgery, and if she'd known something she'd have said, not asked if he'd heard from the surgeon. Wouldn't she? Glancing at his watch, his gut tightened. Over three hours since the nurse had wheeled his mother off to pre-op. What was going on? She should be out and awake and in her own room by now.

He raced to the hospital's main entrance. The automatic doors took their time opening, winding him tighter.

Calm down.

Yeah, right. As if. What if something had gone wrong? Room six was empty. Had her room been changed to another? Blake looked around for someone to ask, anyone. He needed to know what was going on.

Calm down.

Sure thing. As easy as that.

'Blake.' Georgie was walking towards him, calm as could be.

Damn but he was an idiot. So much for the cool, collected doctor he was known to be. He'd been acting like a crazed kid terrified something had happened to his mother. Drawing a lungful, he forced himself to relax. It didn't work. 'Thought you were heading back into Theatre.'

'Shortly.' She took his hand.

Immediately he knew. This was bad. 'What's happened?'

Georgie made to walk along the corridor, then stopped, obviously knowing he was desperate to hear what she had to tell him. 'Firstly, Sarah's going to be all right.'

Steady eyes locked on him. 'She's haemorrhaging, badly. They're getting blood into
her but they haven't been able to stop the
bleeding yet. Andrew's doing everything
possible.' Her hand tightened around his.

He opened his mouth but nothing came
out. Mum was haemorrhaging and they
couldn't stop it.

'Blake, Sarah will get through this. You've
got to be strong.'

Sure thing. Just breathe in and plaster a
smile on his face. Simple as. But Georgie
was right. He'd come home to support his
mother, his family, not to break down like a
gutless wonder. Deep breath. 'Tell me what
you know.'

'Only that the bleeding began after everything had been removed. I'm sorry but Andrew was too busy working on Sarah for me
to interrupt with questions. I shouldn't've
been in there but I saw a nurse taking a
bag of blood into the theatre and as I'd
just scrubbed up for my next procedure I
changed direction and went in to see what
was going on.' Her voice trembled on the
last words. She wasn't as calm as he'd first
thought.

Sweat broke out on his forehead. 'Georgie—' His voice cracked and he stopped.

'It's all right, Blake. I understand. Try to remain calm. I have to go, but I'll be back as soon as possible. I don't want to leave you on your own but I have no choice. My patient's waiting.' She reached up and brushed her lips over his cheek. 'Be strong.'

It took all his strength not to haul her into his arms and hold her close. 'Thanks for coming out to tell me.' Now she'd have to start over with getting scrubbed up. 'See you later.'

'Better believe it.'

Leaning against the wall, he stared at his feet and hauled in deep breaths. Mum was in a serious condition. The surgery would knock her big-time, but adding bleeding to the mix meant she'd have a long road ahead getting back on her feet. If the worst happened and she did have cancer, then she was going to need every last drop of energy and strength to get through the treatments.

'Be strong,' Georgie had said.

She was right. He had to be. He would be. He *was* strong.

* * *

'Thank goodness that's over,' Georgie muttered as she pulled her gloves off and arched her aching back, rubbed hard with her knuckles to ease the kinks.

'I bet that's what your patient will be saying as soon as she wakes up,' one of the theatre nurses said.

'True,' Georgie agreed. She'd just completed a pelvic floor repair after a horrific bike crash caused tears in the muscles. Her patient was worried about her chances of conceiving being affected, but there'd be babies in the future for the woman and her husband.

Her hand touched her own abdomen lightly. What would it be like to give birth to a baby? It wasn't something she'd thought about since the loss of her own baby. Not much anyway, because it hurt remembering those sharp pains as her body rejected the foetus. She'd probably never experience childbirth or being a parent now, unless she changed her mind about having a relationship.

'Anything you need before I head away?' the nurse interrupted her thoughts.

'No, you go. And thanks for your work.' Right, she was out of there. There were patients to see, then hopefully a quiet night with no babies deciding to come early.

'See you tomorrow.'

Tomorrow, another day with more patients needing her undivided attention. It was what she got so much satisfaction from. She couldn't imagine her life being any different, though what it would be like if she did have a baby was a mystery. Not something she'd stopped to think too much about because—because she didn't dare. That would open the floodgates on her emotions, and let the past pour in when she had managed to get it under control so she could lead a normal, if slightly dull, life.

But now uncalled-for longing gripped her. A baby. Small and soft, soaking up all the love she had to give. Totally reliant on her. Yeah, therein lay a concern. Would she be a good mum? She'd like to think so. She'd put everything into trying to be. *And* she had great role models in her parents. A baby, her baby, cuddled against her breast, nuzzling in for sustenance, crying or gurgling. Her heart lurched. This was plain silly. She was single and working all hours as a specialist. On the other side, she was financially set up, had wonderful parents who'd dote on a grandchild and she had a big heart to share. A heart that spent years locked down. But surely it would open up for a baby? It wouldn't be possible to remain remote with her own child. It just wouldn't. She did know how to love, just hadn't been prepared to risk it. Shaking her head to get rid of these dreams she usually denied having, a sigh escaped. Having a baby wasn't happening. Not any time in the foreseeable future. And that future was fast running out in terms of being able to conceive. Tick-tock.

Why, all of a sudden, was she thinking about babies and herself in the same sentence? Nothing to do with patients. It started after seeing Blake for the first time in for ever. Did she really think they might get along so well that she could think about a future with him? When they didn't really know each other very well? Certainly not after they'd grown up and got on with their lives in separate cities.

Blake. He'd be with Sarah by now. The

despair in his face when she gave him the news about his mother's haemorrhage had cut to her heart. He'd been devastated and lost. But he'd begun to rally as she was leaving him. That'd been hard. If only she'd been able to stay and hold him while they waited for more news.

When she entered Sarah's room and saw Blake sitting all scrunched up in a narrow chair watching over his mother as she dozed, any idea of keeping him at arm's length fell away in a blink. She wanted to be there for him. Would he let her? Or, when Sarah was back up on her feet, would he walk away as he'd done from his family once before? 'Hi,' she spoke softly so as not to wake Sarah, who was lying so still the covers weren't moving at all. 'No more bleeding?'

'Not so far. Andrew doesn't think it'll start again, but—'

'But you're going to worry anyway. Fair enough. Want a coffee? I can bring it in here.'

He glanced away as though refocusing away from something that had been worrying him, then looked back to her. 'Spoil me, why don't you?' A slow, tired smile crept onto his face.

'That's a yes-please, thank-you-very-much then? How do you have it?'

'Black and strong.' The smile expanded a bit further. 'Though it's late to be downing coffee.'

'I'm a bit of a caffeine freak. It's my go-to whenever I'm exhausted.' Not good but she'd never claimed to be perfect. 'Be back in a few minutes.' See? She'd had no intention of staying away from Blake, no matter what she'd told herself.

When Georgie returned Sarah hadn't moved at all. She stroked the older woman's hand, and Sarah opened her eyes. 'Hey, hello.'

'Hello,' she croaked.

Reaching for the water, Georgie held the straw to Sarah's lips. 'Try a little.'

Sarah obliged, then turned her face away to look at Blake before her eyes closed again.

Blake was watching his mother like a hawk, worry and love filling his face.

'Has Andrew talked to you about anything else yet?' Georgie wondered if she should be asking, but then she was here as a friend who understood the situation.

Blake spoke slowly. 'He phoned Dad while he was in here with us. There's no sign of cancer. The fibroid came out without any difficulty and has been sent to the lab along with the organs he removed.'

Georgie gave Sarah's hand a gentle squeeze and laid it back on the bedcover. 'That's the best news.'

'It will be even better when the lab endorses Andrew's opinion,' Blake said flatly. Then he seemed to shake himself, and pulled out a wobbly smile. 'It's going to take longer than expected but we've got this.'

Pulling up the other chair, Georgie sat beside Blake and joined him in watching over his mother. He needed a diversion. 'You up for doing Sarah's gardens over the coming weeks?' The Newmans had a large property with stunning gardens. Tidying up the end of the summer debris would be something to keep him occupied when he wasn't in here.

'I'm a dab hand with a shovel these days. Even have some gardens of my own.' Blake looked her way. 'Are you into gardening at all?'

'Believe it or not, I am, but only if it's something I can eat. Growing vegetables is so rewarding that I usually plant enough to feed the whole street. While I like flowers, making gardens for them is a nightmare. I used to try, setting everything out neatly, in order of height and shape, and it would all look wonderful. Then the plants would start growing and there went my design for a pretty garden. Drove me crazy so I gave up and stuck to spuds and peas, and all things green, orange and red.'

'So what do you grow at the front of your house? I'm presuming you're living in a house, not an apartment, if you've got a veg patch.'

'Four-bed bungalow in Merivale. The main lawns and garden are dealt with by the energetic old man next door who loves being outside and needs extra money for his trips to Wellington to see his grandchildren.'

Blake was sussing her out with that deep look she now remembered from days gone by. He used to look at her and her girlfriends like that when he was trying to find a way to get them to invite him and Noah along for a party they were going to. 'That's a large house for one person.'

Hadn't he heard her say she was flying solo last night? Or was she reading him all wrong? That was more likely the case. 'A young girl has been living with me while attending uni, but a couple of weeks ago she moved out to live with her boyfriend.' Georgie smiled. She'd done much the same herself when she and Spenser had fallen for each other in her third year of study. He'd been her first love, but not her last.

'Going to take in another student?' Was that relief slipping across Blake's face? Couldn't be. He wouldn't be interested in her as anything but a family friend, if that. Anyway, she was getting ahead of herself. A man as good-looking and physically attractive as Blake would not be single. Or, if he was between women, it wouldn't be long before there was one hanging on his arm. The thought of which had her feeling flat all of a sudden.

'No idea.' There hadn't been time to do anything about it. Or much enthusiasm, to be honest. She was comfortable living alone, didn't need company just for the sake of it.

Blake glanced at his watch. 'Dad should be here soon. My sisters are coming in after they've fed their kids.'

Georgie stood up. 'I'll get out of the way, leave you to have time together.'

'Not so fast.' Blake stood up beside her. 'I was going to suggest that you and I go somewhere quiet for a meal. It'll get crowded in here when everyone arrives, and I've had hours with Mum to myself.'

'Blake? Are you sure you don't want to be here with them?' Was he doing a runner? Putting space between those he loved and himself because it hurt too much to get close?

'I'm having lunch with the girls tomorrow, and will spend time with Dad later tonight.' He hesitated, seemed to be gathering his thoughts. 'I'd like to spend time with you.'

Her eyes widened. What? Blake just said he wanted to be with her? Her stance softened. 'Sounds like a great idea.'

'There's a restaurant I spotted alongside

the Avon that looks good.' There was a small lopsided smile stretching across those gorgeous lips, and a bit of a sparkle going on in his eyes.

'The River? It's excellent.' She went there often when she'd had a long day and couldn't face preparing something at home. 'I'll leave you with Sarah until your father gets here, and go take a shower and get into some half-decent clothes.' Clothes that she hadn't worn to work, but were hanging in her cupboard for those rare times she had something exciting to do after finishing up here for the day. There was probably a layer of dust on them. 'Back soon.' Had she put her makeup pouch in her handbag that morning?

CHAPTER THREE

'GOOD MOVE, SON.'

'I thought you were asleep,' Blake said through his surprise. Georgie had side-tracked him with her smiles and talk about gardening and he hadn't thought to check if his mother was awake when he suggested dinner. Though it wasn't a problem, he did like to keep different aspects of his life in separate compartments.

His mother's familiar chuckle was filled with exhaustion and not up to her usual vibrancy, but it gave him hope that she was halfway to waking up fully. 'You're both tiptoeing around each other like you're afraid there'll be a conflagration if you get too close. Let loose a bit.' She yawned, as though speaking took what little energy remained out of her.

But more awake than he'd realised. 'You're exaggerating, Mum.' He wanted to laugh at that but it didn't come. Instead he studied his mother, lying against the white bedding. She looked awful, so small and fragile against the white sheets. Nothing like the strong mentor she'd always been for him and his sisters growing up. His heart squeezed.

'I worry about you.' She obviously hadn't finished speaking her mind, but there was nothing new there. 'I'm sure there are women in your life, but I never hear you mention one in particular who tickles your fancy.'

'Old-fashioned term, that.' She wanted him to settle down? Well, guess what? He wasn't ready. Though Georgie seemed to be winding him up some. Okay, and tickling his fancy. So there, Mum. Not that he was telling her.

'You should have children too.'

'Go to sleep, Mum.' He couldn't face that preposterous idea. Adding to the grandchild pool? He wasn't even close to considering parenthood. Too many doubts about his ability to be there when he was needed.

The last thing he'd cope with was failing his child as he had his friend. His hands clenched on his thighs. No way. He'd let Noah down big-time, and who was to say he wouldn't do that again with someone else? If it was his child he failed next time, he didn't know if he'd ever be able carry on. Which was why he never, ever contemplated the idea of having a family one day.

If he'd been able to put Noah's death behind him he wouldn't be having this conversation with himself, or with his mother. Other people managed to move on when they lost someone close to them. Why hadn't he? Had he not tried hard enough? Impossible when every time he closed his eyes at night the first image he saw was Noah. Over the years that had finally faded from his head but the guilt still taunted him whenever he thought about moving on.

An image of Georgie looking sad when Noah was mentioned popped into his head. She hadn't moved on either. He'd bet his late-model car on it. He felt the things that were important to Georgie were similar to those he also thought vital.

A soft snore came from the bed. His

mum had done as he'd told her, though she'd have been fighting the exhaustion to the last flicker of her eyelids.

So she wanted him to have kids? When his sisters already had five between them? Of course she did. Because that would mean he had come in from his self-imposed isolation and settled down with someone he adored. There'd be nothing more she'd like for him. So would he, if only it was possible. He'd thought about children on and off, wondered what it would be like being a dad, but he hadn't put that at the top of his bucket list. Hell, it wasn't even on the list.

'Relax, Blake. Enjoy an evening out with Georgie and stop thinking past midnight. Tomorrow's another day. Enjoy today while you've still got it.'

'So much for thinking you were asleep,' he muttered. 'Seriously, Mum, I don't need your help with Georgie.' What thirty-two-year-old man at the beginning of a wonderful career and living in his own house in a smart suburb needed someone—especially his mother—to start matchmaking for him?

Your success rate in that quarter hasn't been too flash so far.

True. But he hadn't been trying.

'Whatever you say.' Which meant she didn't believe a word he'd said.

He wasn't going to waste time arguing. For one, he never won against his mother, and more importantly, he wanted to enjoy the time here with his parents. He was looking forward to catching up with his sisters and their tribes too. They talked on the phone and had video calls but it wasn't enough. He would like real time with them all. Another first. Usually, on his fleeting visits, he avoided too much contact because it only rubbed in what he didn't have.

A new scent blew into the room. Light floral with a hint of sea breeze. Spinning around he looked at the beautiful apparition standing at the door. Georgie. His heart squeezed painfully. It would take little encouragement to move across and wrap her in his arms, hold her tight against him, breathe deep to absorb more of that scent. Damn it. What was he thinking? 'That was quick.' Her shower? Or his confusion over Georgie?

Tanned shoulders shrugged. 'You know how it is when taking a shower at work. No time for standing under the water absorbing the heat and daydreaming about whatever comes to mind.'

What was rushing to his mind was the vision she'd just painted. Her naked body under steaming water as she tipped her head back and closed her eyes. Her— Stop. Right. Now. That was not a vision he knew. Not of Georgie. One he'd like to see though. His fingers dug into his palms. Damn it, he shouldn't have asked her out for a meal. He wouldn't be able to swallow a single mouthful if those pictures started beating him up. Breathing slowly, he tried relaxing his hands. Think of the mess he'd cleared up on the street yesterday where a dog had gone through a rubbish sack out on the pavement outside his parents' house. Instead his gaze filled with the real vision in front of him with her long dark blond hair free of the knot she'd been wearing it in. 'You look lovely.'

Georgie had changed into a sleeveless white blouse with a pink floral pattern and navy trousers and her feet were ensconced in high-heeled sandals. Pink toenails high-

lighted the navy footwear. Definitely lovely.
Good enough to…

'Thanks.' A faint blush coloured her
cheeks to match that pink shade in her
blouse. 'It's always a bit random when I
get changed into whatever's in my locker.'

He knew what she meant. Though, 'It's
not so bad for me. There're always trousers and a shirt, sometimes a jacket that
matches.'

'Sometimes? Or always? I can't imagine
you not having everything matching. Or
have I made that up? I seem to remember
you were always particular with your clothing.' There was a silly grin expanding over
her mouth, sending spears of lust to his gut.

'You remember correctly.' Now what?
Did they stand here, making idle chatter,
keeping his mother company while waiting
for his dad to arrive? Not that he begrudged
his mother anything, but a sudden pulsing
in his blood was making his feet restless
and his head in need of fresh air.

'Get out of here.' His mother seemed to
be reading his mind.

'There's no hurry,' Georgie said.

Meaning they had all night? Not likely,

Blake thought. Too soon, if it was ever likely they'd spend that much time together. He also intended having time with his dad later. 'Let's go.' Sudden hunger pangs reminded him he hadn't eaten since breakfast. Nothing unusual when he was working, but there'd been loads of time for lunch, only he hadn't been enthused, the worry about his mother weighing too heavy on his mind. He kissed his mother's cheek.

'Have fun, you two. Don't do anything I wouldn't,' his mother whispered.

'Should be a quiet evening then,' he retorted through a strained laugh. His parents knew how to have a right old party when they wanted, so he knew she was teasing. Thank goodness. At the moment the last thing he wanted was a quiet night. At least not a dull, wish-he-wasn't-taking-Georgie-out-because-she-was-scaring-him kind of time. 'Let's get out of here before Mum comes up with any more crazy suggestions,' he said to Georgie and reached for her hand, only stopping from wrapping his fingers around hers as he felt her skin under his fingertips. 'Sorry.'

'No need to be.' Georgie gave him a quick smile.

So she wouldn't have run screaming from the building if he had taken her hand in his? So much for being sensible. Or was it cautious? Didn't matter which, the result was the same. His palm was tingling with anticipation and he was sorry he hadn't carried through on his whim. 'Do we walk or drive?' Those high heels could be uncomfortable for Georgie. But hell, she was beautiful. Always stunning in a happy-go-lucky, daredevil kind of way, now she'd matured into a woman that no man with a heart in his chest or blood pulsing through his body would be able to walk past without taking a deep breath and a longing racing throughout his body.

Not such a new feeling for him. He had felt the same years ago. But never in between. He hadn't really thought about Georgie, preferring to keep her buried along with everything else from that time, otherwise the guilt and despair would pour out of him. He'd promised her father to accept it wasn't his fault Noah had been in the car that crashed into a tree that night. Promised to stop feeling sorry for himself and get on with becoming the surgeon he'd wanted to be. Basically he'd promised not to waste another life. He owed her father big-time for bluntly pointing out how much he had to lose if he didn't pull his act together and stop brooding over Noah's death. And now here he was, thirteen years later, walking alongside Georgie on their way to dinner. Amazing.

'It's roughly three kilometres, and normally I'd say let's walk, but I'm feeling tired after such a long day in Theatre, so do you mind if we drive? We can take my car.'

'I've got Mum's and it's in the hospital carpark. I'm taking you out to dinner so I'll drive.' Hopefully she got it that meant he was paying for dinner too. Even if she'd invited him, he'd be putting his hand in his pocket. It was how he did things.

A gentle nudge from her shoulder on his upper arm, and another, longer smile. 'I'm looking forward to this. I want to catch up on what you've been up to over the years since I moved back up here from Dunedin.'

Blake relaxed. It seemed they were on

the same page over wanting to learn more about each other. 'Bring it on. An edited version, of course.'

'You don't think I want to hear about the wild parties? Or the women you've dated?' That suck-him-in smile had become a wicked grin.

'I was thinking more along the lines of not mentioning what I like for breakfast or what day of the week I do my laundry,' he joked.

She flicked back her hair and laughed. 'This gets better by the minute.'

He held his hands firmly at his sides, avoiding the temptation to run them over those long dark blond waves falling down her back. Until tonight she'd been wearing her hair in a knot at the back of her head, so he hadn't realised how long and shiny it was. It brought memories of longing he'd felt as a teenager when she'd be dressed in a tight-fitting dress that showed off her legs and set his hormones on fire. He hadn't been the only guy who hung out with Noah to think that. She'd been every teenage male's fantasy. Eventually he had moved on, got on with reality in the form of other girls more his age, and had not expected to react to her this way at all.

But there it was. Georgie was making his blood fizz, and his head spin. Perhaps he should hand her the keys so she could drive them safely to the restaurant.

At the car, he opened the passenger door for Georgie, and wanted to slap his forehead.

'What beautiful flowers,' Georgie said and lifted the roses off the seat so she could sit down. 'Did you forget to take them into Sarah?'

'Actually, I bought them for you.'

Her head flipped back and she locked her eyes on him. 'Me?'

He nodded. He'd never bought a woman flowers before. Hell, it had been a long day. He was acting out of line, his usual take-me-or-leave-me attitude nowhere in sight.

A gut-clenching, heart-warming smile lit up her face. 'Thank you. This is starting to feel like a real date.'

He knew exactly what she meant. And it scared the pants off him.

* * *

I'm on a date. Georgie grinned around the fork she'd just slipped into her mouth. *With a really sexy guy.*

When was the last time this had happened? Her mind came up blank.

'The fish's that good?' Blake asked. 'You're grinning like the cat with the cream, a great bowl of the stuff.'

Oops. 'The best snapper I've had in years.'

'Except it's blue cod.'

Double oops. 'Whatever. I'm enjoying it, okay?' The company. The food in her mouth was all but tasteless now that he'd noticed her happiness. But it was fish of some sort, wasn't it? Why couldn't she keep a straight face? Pull on her surgeon's look? Because she didn't want to. She was happy being here with Blake, no longer the pain-in-the-butt teen but an interesting, exciting man she couldn't stop wondering about. What did he do outside of work hours? What was his idea of enjoyment? Were his kisses to die for? Of course they would be. Putting her fork aside she picked up the glass of champagne he'd ordered because they apparently deserved it for getting where they were in their careers. Not quite understanding, Georgie nevertheless took a sip, and smiled some more.

Blake was smiling. It suited him. 'Glad you're having fun.' Then the smile slipped.

Not changing his mind about dinner? That'd really kill the moment. 'What about you?'

He tapped his glass against hers and took a long sip. Then placing the glass back on the table, he reached for her hand, wound his fingers around it and squeezed gently. 'It's been a hell of a day, but being here with you is the best time I've had in ages.'

His smile had a seriousness that snagged at her, and brought a lump to her throat. He meant every word. Or she was hopeless at reading him, and she doubted that. Understanding what people weren't saying when they had lots on their mind was part of her job, and it carried over into everyday life. 'Me too,' she admitted—too easily. 'I feel as though we've always known each other far deeper than is actually true. Strange how that makes me comfortable talking about anything and everything.' Not that they had much, but she wouldn't hesitate once they got started.

'I know what you mean. We hung around in the same places, shared Noah, and yet the age difference, while not huge, was a barrier to talking about a lot of things back then. We were at different stages of our lives. We're grown-ups now and you being older than me means nothing.'

She pressed his hand in reply. 'So we can discuss anything?' There was no stopping the smiles now. 'I like that.' More than liked it. It had been so long since she'd had anyone she could tell whatever was on her mind. She'd become cautious since Noah died. Friends had been quick to support her, talk to her and tell her she'd get over his death soon and not to stop looking forward. After a while they'd become impatient, saying it was time to move on, to stop wishing for the impossible, to accept what had happened. What she had learned to do was stop sharing her heartfelt emotions. No one wanted to know about them. Except her ex-husband and by then she'd forgotten how to talk about the important things. Until now. Somehow it felt as though Blake might have knocked the barriers aside without even trying. Of course she still had to put this to the test. But she believed it wouldn't be hard.

'Even Noah.' There was a load of understanding in his eyes which had to mean he also still hurt over the past.

'I don't feel he's between us as a problem, but more as someone we both cared so much about and just want to be able to remember him without feeling angry or hurt or let down.' Now she was getting serious, and that had the potential to spoil the evening. 'Sorry.'

'Don't apologise,' Blake said softly, still with a smile on that gorgeous mouth that she'd wondered what would be like to kiss. 'Not to me. I get where you're coming from.' Another gentle squeeze and he let go of her hand to cut a piece of his steak and chew it slowly, still watching her.

Blimey, no one had ever got to her so easily, so quickly. What was it about this man? It wasn't in their history, so had to be something she'd not noticed before, or maybe it hadn't even been there. Had he become more understanding of others through learning how his life could be tossed about like a bouncy ball in the wind? Or had he always been this understanding of others? 'Mum and Dad are sorry they won't be catching up with you but they couldn't cancel their trip.'

'No problem.' He paused, then said, 'You know your father came down to Dunedin to see me about six months after the funeral?'

'Never heard of that, but I'd returned to Christchurch by then, hadn't I?'

'You had. He flew down for the day, took me out to lunch and basically told me to pull my head in, stop acting like a misguided youth and get on with my studies because no one was going to wait for me to catch up. Said if I wanted to become a doctor I had to stop wasting the opportunity I had.'

'I can see Dad doing that. But why did he go down there in the first place? How did he know you were having problems? I mean, apart from the fact you were devastated by what happened.'

'Turned out my parents talked to yours one night about how I was missing lectures, drinking too much and generally falling off the rails. It was all true. I'd go out with my mates to the pub and instead of having one beer, I'd have one for me and one for Noah. Not so bad, except I never stopped at one each. I needed more, and since I was having one for Noah each round, I was downing a lot. But worse, if possible, I began lazing in bed instead of going to lectures, and didn't put any effort into studying.' He paused, fixing her with his keen gaze. 'Your father didn't have to say a lot. His words were true and concise, and he woke me up in a hell of a hurry. I got back on track and stayed there without any regrets.' He sighed. 'Other than not being able to have prevented Noah from going out with those idiots that night.'

'Blake, stop it.' Her heart ached for him. 'It was never your fault. Noah wasn't a child. He chose to get drunk, to hitch a ride with a guy who was so far over the limit that it's a wonder he could turn the ignition on, let alone drive.' She reached for his hand, liking the feel of him against her skin. 'You know he could get bolshy if he drank too much, and he had set out to get drunk that night because his girlfriend dumped him.

No one has ever blamed you, or thought you should've been there for him.'

'I get that, but still feel bad. What if I *had* been with him? The outcome of that night might have been different.'

She wouldn't lie. He'd see through that and like her less for it. Which was the last thing she wanted. Blake was fast becoming really important to her and losing him already wasn't happening if she could help it. 'You don't know that, and that still doesn't make it your fault, Blake. It really doesn't. We're responsible for our own actions. Every one of us. Noah owned what happened because he chose to get in that car. End of.' Bad choice of words, but it was how it was. For once she wasn't getting uptight about her loss. For the first time she could talk about it without wanting to curl up in a ball to wait out the pain thinking about Noah brought on.

'To hell with this.' His knife and fork banged down on his plate. 'I need to get out of here, grab some fresh air.'

What? Where did that come from? 'Sure.' She was talking to his back as he strode through the restaurant, his hand pulling his wallet from his back pocket. 'Oh, Blake.' His mother's operation. Then here they were, talking about Noah. No wonder he was upset.

He returned, spoke softly this time. 'Come on. Let's walk a bit. Please?'

Yes, she'd do that. She wanted to be with him, to support him and share the pain and frustration he was going through. And to give a little of herself. Yes, she really wanted to give to Blake, to open up to him. Starting now.

Blake swallowed hard and stared up at the sky. What an idiot. Now Georgie would never want to spend time with him. 'Georgie, I'm sorry.' The day had caught up with him and he'd taken it out on her.

His hand was wrapped in hers. 'I get it, Blake. It's all right.' She began walking, leaving him no choice but to go with her or pull his hand free and turn away which was the last thing he wanted to do.

He kept his mouth shut, for fear of saying something irreparable, like 'I need you.' That'd go down a treat. He wanted her, all of her. To share the fear and pain, and even hopefully help her with moving past the devastation Noah left behind. But most of all, right now, he wanted to hold her close, to breathe her in, to meld with her.

The silence grew, tightened, became heavier. He couldn't stand it any longer. 'Where're you working tomorrow?'

'Public. I've got three surgeries first up, and then consultations in the afternoon.' There was tension in her voice which had nothing to do with what she was saying. 'It never slows down. No sooner do I finish with one patient and there are two more lining up.'

He kept trying for normalcy. It was the only way he was going to get through the next hour. 'I wonder what it's like to have a nine-to-five, five-days-a-week job.'

'I can't begin to imagine it. I love what I do and wouldn't have it any other way. Except on those days when the stress and exhaustion catch up and all I want to do is curl up in the sun with a good book and strong coffee. Which isn't very often,' she added hastily.

A good book, not an exciting man, eh? Interesting. She had said she was on her own but was he missing something here? Like the point being that she needed to be alone on those kinds of days? For him, it was get out amongst it, be busy so his brain could move past what had kept him awake the night before. 'So no regrets with your career choice, even on a bad day?'

She blinked, like she was thinking 'Who is this guy?' 'None at all. Why? Do you have some?'

'Apart from wondering what it might be like to be a commercial fisherman and get to eat fish every single day, no, I'm more than pleased with what I do.'

Finally she laughed. 'Yeah, like I can picture you away at sea for weeks on end, being tossed up and down, smelling of fish, not dressing in your classy clothes.'

Exactly what he'd hoped for. Some of his tension backed off too. 'Put it like that, and you've got a point. Anyway, I'd probably get sick of fish after a while.'

'Do you still go skiing in winter?'

'I belong to a ski club at Ruapehu and try to get down there for a week at least twice a year.' Her question brought back memories of him and Noah skiing at Mount

Hutt and Porters when they were teenagers. Georgie was sometimes there with her girl-friends. Watching Georgie swooping down the mountainside was like watching a ribbon on a light breeze, all soft movements that wound him up hard. 'You?'

She winced. 'I stopped for a few years.' Meaning after Noah died? 'Then when I finally decided to get back into it I couldn't believe I'd left it so long. But to be honest, I haven't done much in a while. There's never a lot of free time.'

All work and no play doesn't lead to an exciting life, Georgie.

Not that he was any better off. All the hiding his heart hadn't brought him any more pain, but neither had it brought happiness. 'Why did you give it up the first time round?'

She stopped walking and turned to look at him. 'I wanted to be safe. For Mum and Dad. And for me.'

There it was. Again. Noah, and how the accident changed them for ever. Blake reached for her hand, covered it with his. 'The ongoing ramifications.' He dipped his head once, then looked back at her, and sighed. 'You didn't want your parents worrying whenever you went to the mountains?'

'No. I didn't. They'd been hurt enough. I wanted to be the strong one for them.'

'And when you want something, you move sky and earth to get it. I knew that was your reason for returning to Christchurch to finish your training, but I guess I didn't think that you'd let it come into other things you undertook.'

'Whereas you didn't return here when you'd qualified as you'd once intended doing. Instead you headed north to establish your career. You needed to stay away from reminders of Noah and why he isn't here any more.'

They knew each other better than he'd realised. 'Two peas in a pod, though with different agendas.'

'Same cause.' Georgie removed her hand, started walking again. 'I believed I was helping my parents by being there for them.'

'And now?' Did she think she might've made a mistake? That she should've continued to study in Dunedin for those last couple of years before returning here? Or then head away to some other city to follow her dream of being a gynaecologist? 'Georgie?'

She was quiet for a long moment. Then she shook her head as though getting rid of whatever was in her mind, and answered him. 'Nothing. I'm good. I made the right choice, no regrets at all.'

'If that's true, then I'm glad for you. It would've been awful if you decided all the hard work had been for something you no longer wanted to do.' However, there was a 'but' behind what she'd said, and for the life of him, he couldn't see what it was. What he did understand was she didn't want to continue talking about it.

Georgie glanced at him. 'So, tell me about the practice you're a partner in.'

In other words, change the subject. He could do that. It might help him breathe easier too. 'You could say I got lucky. A colleague I was specialising with recommended me to her father who's an orthopaedic specialist and a senior partner in Remuera Road Orthopaedic Centre. The partners were looking for a junior partner to take over from John Harris, who'd developed leukaemia and wanted to retire early.'

'Straight from specialising to a partnership. That's pretty darned good.' She sighed. 'We've both done okay.' Wistfulness filtered through her voice.

'Is there something you feel you've missed out on so far?'

'So far? I like that. It puts those erratic dreams in perspective. Because, yes, there are things I want and don't look like I'm within reach of finding. Blimey, now I'm talking too much.' She stared ahead, as if there might be some answers on the path.

'Don't stop.' It was keeping him grounded. 'I want to hear more about who you are, and what you're dreaming of.'

'You want to rekindle our friendship?' Was that hope lightening her eyes?

'You bet.'

'Cool. Works for me. Though rekindle is probably a bit strong. We weren't exactly the greatest of pals back when we first knew each other.' Georgie's shoulder bumped gently against his and she didn't move away, stayed close and personal. Her scent was lightness on the evening summer air, and stirred him deeply. The little things seem to grow, feel big and important. As though he'd come home. Even that idea didn't make him stumble. He had no intentions of ever moving back to Christchurch. He was established in Auckland, comfortable with his lifestyle, engrossed in his career. But Georgie added another dimension to that contentment. He tensed. Breathed deep. Relaxed.

She slipped her arm through his and leaned in a little closer. 'You all right?'

'Absolutely.' Couldn't be better, despite all the questions popping up as they strolled along.

'Do you miss Christchurch at all?'

'Only my family. It would be nice to join in some of the Sunday barbecues at Sumner Beach with my sisters' kids, and drop in on Mum and Dad after work, but it's not as though I don't have anything to do with them. Kat and Dot bring the kids up to my place a couple of times over the year, and I try to get down for birthdays and Christmas.' His sisters made sure he didn't miss out on the important occasions, but it didn't always work out, as he often took on extra work to cover for his colleagues.

'I guess the birthdays are growing in number. Isn't Kat pregnant with her third?'

'Yes. This one was a surprise for her and Bart.' Did Georgie want to have children? Or was she so used to living on her own that the idea of littlies running around set her heart pumping in terror?

'It's kind of funny how some people still manage to get caught out, especially when they obviously don't take chances. I see it quite often with my obstetrics patients. Usually the couples who've planned everything from careers and who'll take time off to the house they buy and prepare for the family are the ones most caught out.' She sounded relaxed, not hyped up over missing out on anything. But then maybe Georgie had become good at hiding her real feelings.

He tested the waters by stretching the truth a little. 'I've never given much thought to the possibility of one day having a family. If I finally settle down with someone it might happen, I suppose.'

'You don't have a ticking clock inside that masculine body.' Her elbow poked him in the waist.

Maybe he did, since he seemed to be thinking about this a bit more since arriving in Christchurch. Since spending time with Georgie, if he was honest. 'Who knows what brings these thoughts on? Not me. I've been too focused on getting on with my career and making my house a home to consider that the years are going by at an alarming rate.'

'Now you're sounding like an old man,' she said with a laugh, and leaned closer as they walked past a low-hanging tree.

He tucked his arm tighter around hers, absorbing her warmth and softness. When he thought about that, it had been a long time since he'd felt quite so at ease with another person. 'Thank you for being here for me.'

Georgie's head flipped up and suddenly those beautiful eyes were locked on him as she placed both hands on his upper arms. 'I couldn't stay away.'

Thump. His heart slammed into his ribs. Her eyes were wide and dark, and filled with something he was afraid to believe. Longing. For him. He couldn't drag his gaze away from them. Nor could he step back from her body and her aura. He had to stand close, to breathe deep, to feel her heat, her kindness and sense of fun. 'Georgie.' He breathed her name out. 'Georgie.'

Heat seared his cheek where her knuckles caressed softly. 'Blake. I don't know what's happening but I want to kiss you,' she whispered. 'To be kissed *by* you.' Her fingertip traced his lips, seductive with the light touch.

He stood still, fighting the need to haul her into his arms and kiss them both senseless. Damn but he wanted her. So he had to turn away. Except he couldn't. Make that wouldn't. He always walked away. He'd gone away from family and friends to hide his guilt, to start over. He'd held back with women for fear he'd hurt them, or be hurt. Which he could do to Georgie. But not if he gave her everything he had.

Her hand fell away. 'I get the picture.'

Blake reached for her, pulled her up close, lowered his mouth to hers. 'No, you don't.' Kiss now, talk later. The moment he felt those soft lips under his, he knew there'd be no talking for a while to come. Kissing Georgie was like falling into a cushion of air that floated in one spot. Warm, hot, sensational, exhilarating. And most of all, Georgie was putting him back together again. All the doubts he'd carried for so long were evaporating so fast he couldn't keep up. 'Georgie,' he whispered between their mouths before plunging his tongue into her warmth to taste, to feel, to know her.

Then she pulled away.

His heart plummeted. 'Georgie?'

She squeezed his hand. 'Take me home.'

Georgie had the door open before the car stopped rolling up her drive, her house key in her hand. That kiss had woken a demon inside her. She'd been kissed before, even had some amazing kisses, but Blake's were a whole new level of wonder. They were filling her with hope and joy, and desire so strong she would've been in a heap at his feet if she wasn't clinging to him so tightly when they were kissing. And loving the feel of his firm muscles under her palms, against her breasts, around her waist. Every last bit of Blake was waking her up in ways she hadn't known before.

He was right on her heels as she shoved the door open. Stepping inside he pushed it shut and turned to take her in his arms. 'Hey.'

'Hey, yourself,' she whispered, watching him closely, looking for doubt or regret. He might not want this, might've decided on the way here to drop her off and head away. But he'd followed her inside.

'Georgie.'

Here we go. He's going say goodbye.

She waited for the crunch to come.

Blake reached for her, pulled her in against that long body and held her tight. 'I need you,' he whispered. 'I need you.'

No words could express the desire flooding her. Nothing but action could show him her need. Tipping her head back she stretched up and found his mouth with hers, began to kiss him with everything she had. This was what had been missing in her otherwise happy life. This was what could turn her world into amazing and thrilling and be the most important reason for waking up each morning. She needed this too

Slow down, Georgie. You've only just caught up with Blake.

Which was exactly why she didn't want to go slow. Too many years had been lost.

Years when she'd had no idea Blake was her match. She knew that now? Deep inside, yes, she believed she did. But of course it wasn't going to be that straightforward. Even if they went any further than this. Despite these feelings of wonder and desire filling her, she understood there were two of them in this picture to make decisions. She could also be totally wrong. Blake might kiss every woman like this, as if there were no tomorrow.

His mouth left hers, slowly, the absence excruciating even when she could still feel him on her mouth. 'I need you, Georgie.' The hope and longing and even pain in his gaze undid the last knots inside her.

'Touch me.'

He proceeded to do that. His hands were under her blouse, her bra, covering her breasts, teasing her nipples. His thighs against hers as he backed her up against the wall. And his tongue was circling her mouth, tasting, teasing, winding her tighter and tighter.

Heat poured throughout her body as she tore his shirt free of his trousers and ran her fingers over his hot skin, across his chest, down his back, undoing his belt and zip, back over his buttocks and around to his manhood. As she touched him, he was touching her, and her world came in to this—the heat and longing. Blake. And only Blake.

She froze as he pulled his mouth away, then smiled as he bent down for his trousers now around his ankles. 'Wait. Condom.' Stepping out of them he tugged his wallet out of the pocket and pulled a packet free. He had the condom on so fast she knew he was as ready as she was. And somewhere along the way she had removed her panties, and wound her legs around his waist to accept him. And Blake was pushing into her, and she was taking him and then—and then she was coming and crying out and exploding with desire and touching him and feeling him coming and hearing his roar before he shuddered his release inside her.

He held her tight, his chest rising and falling fast, his breath hot and sharp against her neck. Her head spun, her heart raced and warmth filled her, reaching to every corner, bringing her alive in ways she hadn't known in for ever.

Eventually Blake straightened, set her

gently on her feet. 'Georgie,' he whispered. 'Where have you been?'

'Waiting for this, I think.' Talk about honesty. It might be too much for both of them, but she couldn't take the words back. Leaning back in his arms, she looked up at him. 'I don't know what's going on, Blake. I only know I don't want to bolt to my safe place just yet.'

His face was inscrutable as he looked down at her.

Her skin tightened. She'd gone too far, said too much. Being open and honest was new for her, yet the words had poured from her, riding on the wave of desire.

Blake took her face in his hands. 'Thank you for being honest.'

So he had heard her clearly. 'Just a little.' She wasn't about to forget those kisses or the desire that had ignited within her.

He placed the softest kiss ever on her swollen lips. 'Georgie, I don't know where I'd be without you these past two days.'

Her throat blocked with emotion. It hurt to see how vulnerable he was. This was Blake as he'd become the night Noah died.

Before she could speak, Blake's phone

rang. As he apologised and retrieved his phone from his trouser pocket, she stepped sideways and reached down for her blouse. Too little too late, but suddenly she felt vulnerable. She had to remember that they hadn't made each other any promises. They'd made love, and now that was over.

Blake hung up. 'That was my dad. I think he needs to talk.'

Reality check, or an escape route? She finished dressing, trying not to let him see how his words stung. 'Sure, I understand.'

To cover her confusion, she directed him to the bathroom, then headed to the kitchen to make coffee.

Hip against the counter, arms folded under her breasts, she stared at the floor and wondered what was going on in her life. In little more than a day she'd become so much closer to Blake, and she didn't want to step away. There was a pull she couldn't deny. She had dropped all caution and followed through on the need and hope filling her, when maybe she did need to slow down. A little anyway. It wasn't like her to leap in without checking the bottom of the pool first. At least it hadn't been for a long time. So why start now?

Because she wanted to take a chance on Blake. Only Blake. She had no idea why he was waking her up so fast. He just did. As though his reappearance in her life was bringing the past and future together with a hell of a bang. She should be hauling on the brakes and aiming for slow and careful. But she couldn't. She'd done that for too long. The urge to get out there and really start living was grabbing her, shaking her roughly. Telling her it was time to get on with making her dreams come true before it was too late. Dreams she'd filed away when her brother died and she'd come home. Her parents had been getting on with living in the present for a while now. They didn't need her hanging around making certain everything was all right. They'd become her excuse for not risking her heart. Blake had started this. Had he always been lurking in the back of her head, her heart, waiting for an opportunity to step up into her life? Unlikely, but stranger things happened.

'Georgie, you all right?' Blake stood before her, his clothes back on straight, worry flowing out from those grey eyes. 'I don't want to hurt you.'

'I know.' She hoped she was right. 'Look, your dad needs you. You'd better get going'

He reached for her then, kissed her lightly. A kiss that didn't have the passion of a short while ago, but still held something special that made her step up to that wonderful body and hold him tight.

'I'll see you tomorrow.' There was relief in his voice. Had he been worrying she mightn't be patient with him?

'Goodnight, Blake. Take care and try to get some sleep.'

CHAPTER FOUR

'MORNING, SARAH. HOW did you sleep?' Georgie entered the room looking a damned sight better than Blake was feeling. But then he'd barely managed an hour's sleep throughout the long night. The moment the birds started their early morning tweeting ritual he had clambered out of bed and gone for a run around Fendalton, trying to find the answers to all the confusion in his head that hadn't been forthcoming during the night. Again he came up with nothing.

But he had found the familiar streets and houses soothing. The paintwork and gardens had changed since he'd lived here, some houses had been added onto, a couple had been torn down and replaced which was most likely due to damage in the earthquake years back. But mostly it was like fitting into an old, comfortable skin as he'd jogged along the sidewalks. To think he'd been in a hurry to get out of town when he headed to university, and now it was as though he was being beckoned to stop and look harder, to come back and slot into the place he'd left so fast. As if that'd be possible. No one could go back, only forward. The people he'd known back then had moved on, either to other places or with their careers and families.

His gaze shifted left to Georgie. Did his forward include the woman making his heart tap a little faster than usual? He watched her watching his mother.

'In between the nurses taking my BP and checking up on everything I slept like a log.' His mother's smile was tired, as was everything about her.

Now he looked closer, he could see shadows under Georgie's eyes and some tension at the corners of her mouth. Not relaxed as she had been in his arms kissing him senseless last night. Not like the hot woman who'd turned him on so fast he hadn't known if he was coming or going. No pun meant. There'd been tension in his muscles during those kisses and their lovemaking, but this morning a different tension was making him uneasy, preventing him from letting go of the fear gripping him.

'Pain level?' Georgie asked his mother.

She sighed. 'Honestly? Seven out of ten.'

'Honest is best.' Georgie brushed a kiss on his mum's cheek. 'Andrew asked me to drop by and check on you. He's coming along later, but he got called to an emergency during the night and is currently at home grabbing a couple of hours' sleep.'

'Seems everyone's missing out on that.' Blake pushed to his feet and crossed to give Georgie a quick hug. Roses wafted under his nose. He closed his eyes and breathed in some more. Red came to mind. Like the large, double blooms that had grown in his mother's garden for as long as he could remember. 'Good to see you, Georgina.'

A soft chuckle came to him. 'No one calls me that any more.'

'It's been a long time, I know.' As thirteen-year-olds he and Noah had used to chant 'Georgina… Georgina…' when they wanted to wind her up and get her attention. Definitely childish, but it worked a treat every time. 'But at least you haven't gone into a huff this time.'

'I can if you want me to.' Her smile was real, despite the strain in her eyes.

'Save it for another day.' He stepped back. 'Are you going to examine Mum? If so, I'll go and get us all some coffee.'

Georgie shook her head. 'No, that would be stepping outside the ethical boundaries. Andrew suggested that since I was coming in to see Sarah anyway I could make sure she's comfortable and there's no indication of further bleeding. He's ordered a coagulation screen to see if there's a deficiency of one of the clotting factors.' She gave him a smile that told him all was well between them. 'But feel free to get that coffee. I could do with another caffeine hit before I head off to Public. And a croissant with jam and chocolate if you're going to the cart outside the main entrance.'

'I am now. Back shortly.' There was a spring in his step as he left the room and headed down the corridor to the entrance and the coffee cart beyond. As hollowed out as he felt over his mother, Georgie seemed to light a spark within him. She'd been there for him last night in more ways than he could ever have imagined, and here she was again, checking in on Mum and letting him know she had his back.

'There you go, two cappuccinos and a long black.' The woman at the cart handed him a cardboard tray and a paper bag of croissants. 'Enjoy.'

He blinked. Where had his mind been? 'We will, thanks.' He was hungry this morning. Less than half a dinner and then the activity at Georgie's had caught up with him.

When he reached his mother's room he heard her saying, 'All my abdominal area hurts, especially when I roll over or sit up.'

'That's normal,' Georgie replied. 'Your muscles took a hit when Andrew operated, and don't forget he had to go back in a second time. The wound's approximately twelve centimetres long so he was able to remove the fibroid without damaging it and leaving behind a potential problem with cells floating around.'

'I expected pain, but not quite this level.' Just then his mother caught sight of him standing in the doorway. 'Come in, Blake. We're done with the medical talk.'

By the look on her face, Georgie didn't think so, but she shrugged. 'That coffee smells good. Just what I need.'

'Glad to be of use.' He handed her a cardboard cup with a smile. 'What time do you need to get to Public?'

'Five minutes ago.' She was smiling right back at him.

Sending his stomach into a riot. 'Then you'd better take that coffee and food with you.' He'd been hoping for a few minutes with her, but understood all too well how little time surgeons had first thing in the morning. That she'd dropped by at all meant a lot. And put to rest any concerns she mightn't want to see him after what went on between them last night.

'I'm about to.' She was watching him, still smiling, but there appeared to be a question she didn't know how to put into words hovering in the background. When she finally looked away, it was at his mother. 'You take care, Sarah, and do everything the staff tell you to. Make the most of being looked after.'

'You really think I'll be allowed to do a darned thing once I get home? There's not only Alistair to tell me what I can and cannot do, Blake will have more than his say when it comes to when I eat, breathe and move.'

'You're so right, and you'll love every moment of it.'

'True.'

His mother wasn't going home any time soon. Not when she looked like she'd been run over by a bus, and moved as though it had been a double decker that knocked her out. Not until there was colour in her cheeks, and the pain had diminished to almost nothing. Definitely not until Andrew and his team had found out what the hell was wrong with her. 'I'm extending my stay to include next week, Mum.' At least that long, and possibly longer, depending on how everything panned out with her.

'You don't have to do that, son.'

Yes, he did. Besides, 'I want to.' The look of pure love on his mother's face nearly did him in. He was only doing what any son would do, but then he hadn't been around for most things in the past so she was no doubt pinching herself under that bedcover. 'I mean it.'

Right then a nurse strolled in, a container of pills in one hand and the pulse metre in the other. 'Morning, Sarah. I see you've had a restless night.'

Georgie stepped aside. 'I'll get going. See you later?' She looked to him.

Yes, please. 'How about we go out for a meal? Give the Ale House a go?'

'I'd like that. What about Alastair? He could join us, if you think he wants some company. I can share you.' She smiled.

'I'll ask him.' It would be good having his dad there too. They weren't used to spending a lot of time together though. Now was the time to fix that. 'He might want to come here, and catch up with me at home later though.'

'Play it by ear then. Shall I meet you at the pub?' She sounded eager to spend more time with him, which took away any doubts he'd felt when he'd had to leave her so quickly last night.

'There's good.' Bring it on. But first there were tests and scans and discussions with the specialist to be dealt with. And the answers to assimilate, good or bad. Blake gulped his coffee and sat down beside his mother to while away the hours until the day could really begin.

What to wear? Georgie did a mental flick through her wardrobe as she drove home from work. That new sky-blue top brought out the blue of her eyes and looked good when she let her hair down over her shoulders. What about the pretty blouse with a light blue and pink flower pattern that accentuated her slim face and throat? Or the red-and-white-striped dress?

She actually laughed. She felt so darn good after last night, despite Blake's abrupt departure. At first she'd been a bit miffed, but reality kicked in, reminding her that he had a lot on his mind and most of it had nothing to do with her and their love-making. But this new feeling of happiness was still Blake's fault. She didn't usually go around laughing over nothing. But this wasn't nothing. This was her letting her hair down and reaching out to have fun. Personal fun that involved a man. A spunky man who turned her on just thinking about him. Last night she'd been wearing a simple pink and white blouse and navy trousers, and they'd been going to a more upmarket restaurant. Those had been the clothes in her locker at the hospital, and not once had she felt uncomfortable. So why all this palaver about what to wear to the Ale House?

Because it had nothing to do with the destination and all to do with the company she'd be keeping. She wanted Blake to see her at her best. Hopefully looking sexy. She was letting someone in, undoing the knots holding her heart closed, taking a risk on caring about someone who might hurt her. Looking sexy had to help.

She'd hurt her ex more than he had her. All because of those knots and the fear of losing someone close to her again. Like her unborn baby. That's how she had lost Tommy and became even more determined to look out for herself. Until Blake turned up. And now all caution had floated out the window. She wanted more of Blake, of life, of everything.

The red and white dress for sure.

When she saw Blake's eyes widen and his mouth lift in a sexy smile as she pulled up outside the pub that night, she knew she'd made the right choice. Her toes tightened and her skin tickled, while inside her chest there was quite the pounding going on. Had she ever felt like this? Of course she had. Hadn't she? When she fell in love last time she'd been thrilled and excited, but there was something more to Blake. Sexy, drop-dead good-looking, serious and funny, focused yet able to step beyond being a surgeon. Whatever it was, Blake was different to any man she'd known and she wanted to grab him with both hands and never let go. Which was such an about-face from her usually reticent approach to men and relationships it should be scaring the pants off her. She wriggled her hips. Knickers were firmly in place. She might not know him well, but she understood what had driven him over the last thirteen years. 'Hi.' Leaning in close, she kissed his cheek.

He moved so their lips met. His kiss was light and short and thrilling. Pulling back, he gazed at her with something like relief. 'It's good to be with you. Dad's not joining us. He's sitting with Mum, and it'll take a bulldozer to shift him before lights out.'

'As long as he doesn't think I wouldn't want him with us. He must be so worried though.'

'Very.' As Blake sounded. 'And he said to say he'll join us on another occasion, when Mum's doing better.'

'Good. How was your day?' she asked.

'The sisters visited Mum and then dragged me out for lunch. Man, can they talk.'

'No wonder you look exhausted,' she teased.

He took her arm. 'I booked a table by the window. What would you like to drink?'

'A Pinot Gris would be lovely.' She sank onto the chair he held out. 'You enjoyed catching up with your sisters then?'

He sat beside her, not opposite. That had to be a good sign. 'You bet. They gave me a hard time about still being single and able to do whatever I like, but there's nothing unusual in that. I had to wade through hundreds of photos on their phones of the kids playing on the beach, bouncing on the trampoline, eating takeaways. You name it, they were doing it.'

'And you loved every photo.'

Blake was trying to be aloof but his mouth

curved upwards and there was a sparkle in his eyes for the first time in a while. 'I think a new photo file's being sent through to me in the next few days.'

A waitress arrived with her wine and handed both of them menus. 'Today's special is pork belly. I'll give you a few minutes to decide.'

What was the rush? The place wasn't crowded. Georgie picked up the menu and opened it. 'I am indulging, eating out twice in one week.'

'I haven't left town yet. We could up the number quite a bit.' Blake's hand briefly touched her thigh. 'What are you doing tomorrow night?'

'You tell me.'

What about kissing you again?

Making love, this time slowly, getting to know each other's needs a little more. She reached for her glass, took a careful sip. How to stop the heat invading her cheeks?

'Yeah, well, who knows what tomorrow will bring.' He'd gone all serious in an instant.

'Want to talk about today's tests?' she asked quietly. She spied the waitress already heading in their direction and waved her away as they chatted about Sarah's condition.

'Blake, I know you're worried sick. Of course you are. We all are. But remember, Sarah's in good hands.'

He nodded. 'I know. And thank you for listening to me being so gloomy. I am sorry for being such a pain.'

'It's okay. Any time you want to talk, I'm here to listen, as long as you reciprocate if needed.' She meant it.

'No problem.'

'Want to decide on a meal?' She slid a menu across. 'We're getting evils from our waitress.'

'Tough.' He pushed the menu away. 'Tell me about your day.'

Georgie settled back in her chair and went with the flow. If he wanted to wind down, then she was all for it. It might bring them even closer.

'Dad'll be home by now, I guess. Probably wishing he could stay with Mum all night,' Blake said as he and Georgie walked towards her car after dinner.

'Have they always been so close?'

'Absolutely. They had a rushed wedding because I was on the way but always reckoned it was the best thing to happen.' Blake paused, smiled to himself. 'They've always been very loving with each other as far back as I can remember.' Hadn't they? His smile dimmed. When he'd been about ten there'd been some heated arguments behind the bedroom door, and frosty weeks when neither of his parents were very talkative. 'I suppose all relationships have their off times.'

'Mine certainly did.'

'How long were you married?' He'd felt sad when he heard through his parents that she'd split up with her husband, thinking how she didn't need any more grief in her life.

'A little over three years.'

Mindful that he was setting himself up to have to answer some personal questions further on, Blake followed through on the need to know more about Georgie and why she was single when she'd always been so popular with the guys. 'Do you think Noah's passing had anything to do with it?'

'Yes. I wasn't as ready as I thought.' The words were clipped.

Blake felt the pain behind them. It was exactly why he avoided getting deeply involved with a woman. Except things were changing within him since he'd met up with Georgie again. Taking her hand in his as they continued along the pavement, he waited to see if she'd expand on what she'd said.

Her fingers squeezed his. 'When I fell for Tommy I believed I was open to love, could love him as much as he loved me.' She paused.

They'd reached her car and Blake stood with Georgie as she stared around.

'I tried. I really did. But it wasn't enough. I was afraid of losing someone I cared so much for again.' Looking up at him, she blinked softly. 'Instead I hurt Tommy.'

Without hesitation Blake wrapped his arms around Georgie and rested his chin on the top of her head. 'Which in turn hurt you.' He rocked back and forth on the balls of his feet, his hands splayed across her back, feeling the trembling in her body. 'It's okay, Georgie.'

Her head lifted enough so she could look at him. 'No, it's not. I inflicted the sort of pain I was trying to avoid for myself. That's selfish.'

'You didn't go into the relationship just for yourself though, did you?' He couldn't believe she was telling him this, and yet maybe it wasn't such a surprise given how well they'd been getting on right from the moment they'd met up at the clinic. It wasn't as though they hadn't talked quite a bit since then. Plus there was a definite empathy about the past resonating between them.

'Of course not.' Her head dropped to his chest, pressed against him. 'Not as far as I was aware anyway.'

He nodded, then leaned down and placed a light kiss on those beautiful lips that he hadn't been able to put out of his mind since he'd kissed them last night. 'We have known each other a long time, haven't we? Better than I'd realised, I think.'

She smiled and pressed her mouth to his, deepening the kiss to a full-blown, heat-him-up-fast connection.

'Georgie, Georgie.' He groaned and pulled

her in closer, so close she felt as though she was a part of him. And then he began kissing her back, giving her everything he had. How had he lived without her? She made him come alive by being herself. A different woman to that fast, crazy one he'd been in lust with years ago, but equally enthralling and exciting. Although more grounded now, which wasn't a bad thing. Was he ready for wherever this might lead?

Didn't know, didn't care right now. His mouth fully claimed Georgie's, and his tongue slipped inside that warm moist place to taste and fill him with wonder.

'Get a room,' a male voice cut through the haze in his head.

In his arms Georgie stiffened, pulled back and looked around. 'Now there's a thought.'

Blake grinned down at her. 'You think?' After she'd been talking about her failed marriage only minutes ago? Despite making love last night, this *was* happening too fast. Last night had been about destressing and not fighting the heat between them. For him anyway, and Georgie had been as fast to react to him as he her, so that had to

mean she had similar feelings about him.
Didn't it? He hoped so. He'd show her more,
give her more. Tonight would be more personal. Georgie needed to know what she
was doing, where she was going, or she'd
get hurt. So he knew what he was doing,
did he? Nope. Not a clue. He only knew
that holding Georgie close, kissing her and
wanting more, was driving him on a one-
way road and that he didn't want to turn
back. Not yet. How about having a fling? It
could be the best of both worlds for them,
if Georgie felt the same. They'd definitely
have fun if last night was anything to go by,
and maybe along the way they could sort
out what it was they were really looking
for, could find out if this could go further
and become something special and lasting.

'I'm thinking I haven't got a clue, but I'm
letting go some of the hang-ups that have
kept me uptight and on a very narrow path
for so long it's embarrassing.' She stretched
up on her toes and kissed him. 'Let's go
back to my house for a coffee and see how
things unfold.' Then she blinked, as though
she'd just realised what she'd suggested. A

light laugh crossed those gorgeous lips. 'I'm not good at this.'

'You are more than good. Try amazing.' He opened the car door. 'Come on, get in. I'll follow you home and then we'll see how we're feeling.' Ten minutes cool-down time wasn't a lot, but sometimes all it took to change a mind was sixty seconds of common sense filtering into an overheated head.

Her smile cut straight through to his heart, opening him up wide, and allowing too many emotions to rip free. Georgie really was beautiful, and exciting, and so many other wonderful things he had yet to learn about. Her laughter tightened his groin so hard he was never going to be able stand up straight again. Nor was there much likelihood of common sense finding him.

She'd put one foot in the car when bells sounded. A phone. Not his.

Georgie removed hers from her bag and stared at the screen, dismay removing the laughter from her face. 'I suspect this is just what the doctor didn't order.' Putting it to her ear, she said, 'Hello, Georgie Price speaking.' A pause. Then, 'How far apart are her contractions?'

Blake waited, the tension slowly ebbing from his groin when he'd believed nothing would fix it other than making love to Georgie. The chances of which were rapidly heading down the road as he listened to her end of the conversation.

'I'll be there shortly. Tell Anna not to panic.' *Yet*, she added after she'd hit the red button on the phone's screen. 'You heard that?' she asked.

'Who'd be an obstetrician, eh?'

She touched his arm softly. 'I'm sorry. More than I can tell you, actually.'

Her cheek was warm under his thumb. 'The timing stinks, but it could've been worse.'

'It's probably the first time I've regretted being a doctor.' Her smile was wobbly.

'Then you need to get out more.' He grinned. 'What are you doing this weekend? Babies and urgent surgeries not counted.'

'Spending time with you, I hope.'

Perfect answer. 'How about we go to Akaroa for the day?'

Go on. Put it out there. The idea's churning your stomach anyway. No matter what her reply, it can't get any worse.

'Or we could stay over for the night?' She might change her mind about being with him once she had time to think about where they'd been headed tonight. It could've been an impulsive reaction to suggest going home that she'd regret later. Whichever, he needed to say what was on his mind. 'You don't have to decide now. I'll talk to you tomorrow.'

'I'd like a night away with you.'

As quick as that. His breathing eased for the first time since he'd taken her in his arms. 'Leave everything to me.'

'Believe it or not, I was going to.' Her smile was almost shy. It *had* been a long time for her.

But then it had for him too. He wasn't counting the casual liaisons he'd experienced over the last few years. They meant nothing other than brief enjoyment with lovely women. Come to think of it, there hadn't been any serious relationship since he was nineteen. It was time to do something about that. Step one. Spend the weekend away with Georgie.

Then her smile slipped. 'Wait. What about

Sarah? You won't want to be away overnight while she's still laid up.'

'It's a modern world. We have phones. Plus Dad wants to hog Mum all to himself when he's not at work.' He'd get in touch so often his parents would probably block his number. 'I wouldn't go if I didn't think they'd tell me if anything goes wrong. Besides we'll only be little more than an hour's drive away.' Not long ago he'd thought five minutes was too far away. He was changing. Georgie was changing him.

'If you're sure.'

'I am.' He could relax with Georgie like no one else. 'Keep in touch once you know how this delivery's going.'

'It could take for ever, but as Anna's only at thirty-four weeks, I don't think baby has any intentions of taking his time. Prems don't seem to like hanging around inside when they've made up their mind to meet mum.'

'Fingers crossed this one does.' Blake laughed. It didn't matter if he had to wait twenty-four hours, he'd be there when Georgie was finished with work and ready to relax. Then they'd go away for the weekend. 'Bet you've got a busy schedule tomorrow as well.'

Georgie smiled. 'Of course. While you'll be watching over Sarah all day.'

'True.' He couldn't be disappointed. If not for his mother needing surgery he mightn't have caught up with Georgie in the first place. It was the best thing to come out of the whole nightmare involving his mother. 'See you tomorrow. Take care.'

She brushed a light kiss over his mouth. 'You too.'

'You realise tomorrow's the anniversary of when Noah left us?' Georgie asked on the way to Akaroa on Saturday morning as Blake drove out of the cheese factory premises where they'd bought a selection of the famous cheeses to nibble later on.

'I do.' His reply was sharp.

Shouldn't she have mentioned it? But how could she not when it was such a part of who she was now? Bet it was the same for Blake, even if he didn't want to admit it. 'Thirteen years. A long time, yet sometimes it doesn't seem so.'

'Yes.' Softer tone this time.

'I don't know what you think, but I believe we're on the same page over Noah and how badly we were both hurt.'

Blake placed a hand on her thigh and gave her a rueful smile. 'Georgie, I'm sorry. I didn't mean to be so abrupt. Keep talking about him. Please.'

'Not if it upsets you.' But then that was back to hiding and she'd started moving away from those reactions. He needed to too. 'I don't know why but being with you has made it easier to talk about him for the first time ever.' Not that they'd actually spoken much regarding Noah, but she'd begun to feel she could if she wanted to. When she did she didn't want Blake making it difficult.

'It's been a taboo subject for so long I automatically pull down the shutters, even now when I'm feeling more relaxed than I ever have about him. This is good for me, and hopefully for you. In this together, so to speak.'

'Absolutely. I understand what you're saying. It's like me thinking my actions were to protect Mum and Dad when I now accept it was all about hiding my own pain.

Plus my fear of being hurt so much again.' She glanced across to her friend. Yes, they were definitely friends, no matter what. 'Since you turned up in my life again it's as though a huge weight has lifted. I'm no longer feeling crushed.'

Blake pulled the car off the road and killed the motor before turning to take her hands in his. 'That would have to be the loveliest thing I've heard in for ever. Thank you. I'm starting to have similar feelings about everything.' He leaned close enough to kiss her, gentle yet exhilarating.

Georgie closed her eyes and accepted his kiss as though she'd never been kissed before. It gave her a sense of kindness, wonder and relief all rolled in together. It was as though she'd finally landed on her feet, had found what she'd been searching for over the last thirteen years without knowing what she was doing. 'Blake,' she whispered between them. 'I'm glad you came home.'

Blake kissed her lightly. 'I'm glad I came to town too. Otherwise I'd never have got this close to you. I am so thankful to you for being there for all of us, and more so for how we seem to be getting along so well.'

'It's been a bonus, for sure.' She touched his face. 'I want to move forward. I want to stop thinking about Noah and what I lost every time I get close to someone. I want to throw myself into this with you and just enjoy.'

'A fling with Georgie Price. Who'd have believed it?' He kissed her again. 'Bring it on.'

'Starting right now.' It was as much as they could have, given they lived in different parts of the country with career positions that neither would want to give up. A shadow crossed over her. Already she felt sad not to be able to look forward to a future together that involved more than getting together occasionally for fun and lovemaking. But better to be practical than unrealistic. And happy rather than sad.

Sitting back in his seat he reached for the ignition and tossed her a heart-melting grin.

'You're ready for some more fun then?'

'Bring it on.' They were on the road, heading to the beginning of something wonderful. That's how she'd look at this adventure. A fling was just what this doctor was prescribing, as of now.

'Good idea.' He was sounding relaxed again.

Georgie looked out at the passing scenery, glad to be moving again, heading in the direction of that fun he'd mentioned with a cheeky look in his eyes. They were getting closer, and neither of them knew where that might ultimately lead. At the moment they would make the most of what they had. Blake didn't live here and wouldn't be staying on any longer than necessary to see Sarah back on her feet, but that didn't mean they couldn't make the most of what time they did have and get to know each other on a new and deeper level. She would not waste time wondering where that might lead, because then she'd have to remind herself there could be heartache to come, and for the first time in years she did not want to consider that. It would put a dampener on letting go and making the most of time spent with Blake.

'How about we start with a walk along the wharf,' Blake said as he drove down the short main street lined with old French-style houses and shops.

'Fine with me.' She looked out at the fairly calm sea. 'There's no wind to toss my sunhat into the tide.' Yesterday when she'd stopped at the mall to pick up a new printer she'd ordered she'd gone past a clothing shop where there was a display of sunhats. A wide brimmed straw hat with a wide yellow bow had caught her eye and she'd had to have it. The yellow matched the cream and yellow top she was wearing with mid-blue three-quarter-length trousers.

'Don't ask me to dive in and retrieve it if that happens,' Blake laughed.

'I thought you were a gentleman,' Georgie laughed back.

When Blake parked, he was out of the car and opening her door before she'd gathered her hat and bag from the back seat. 'Allow me, madam.' He grinned.

'Cheeky so-and-so.' Georgie plopped a kiss on his cheek, except he turned enough that her mouth covered his, and the kiss went from light to intense. When Blake's arms wrapped around her, her body moulded to his in an instant, and she forgot everything but Blake. The feel of him, his scent, his mouth on hers.

Then he was pulling back just enough to look into her eyes. 'Georgie, you make me so happy.'

Her chest ached where her breath caught. 'Ditto.'

'Good.' He gave her another kiss, shorter, less intense this time, and took a step back, his hands sliding slowly from her back to her arms, to her wrists, before he took one hand in his and turned towards the wharf along the way.

His hand was strong and firm, making hers feel soft and feminine. His upper arm brushing her shoulder as they strolled along the jetty had her feeling small and cosy. Even protected. Most of all, it was happiness filling her throughout, bringing a smile to her mouth, a smoothness to her raw edges, putting a spring in her step. She knew there was a real possibility she'd get hurt. If she fell too hard and too deep.

Then don't.

She'd have fun, make the most of what was on offer, give as good as she got and then move on. At least she might be free of the fear that had held her locked in a solo state for so long. Free or tied down even tighter with more pain?

A deep sigh slid across her lips. She was not going back there. It was barely days since she'd started letting go of the past, but once the knots started loosening everything seemed to be rushing at her. She would be strong, and look forward, no matter what. She was over staying in the wings, watching life pass by. If they were only going to have a fling, then she'd grab every moment, no regrets allowed. Except already she was beginning to question whether she only wanted a fling. Sure there'd be obstacles to anything more, but surely they could overcome those if necessary?

Blake stopped walking and pointed out beyond the end of the wharf. 'Are those dolphins out in the middle of the harbour?'

Georgie focused on what was important and let the questions fall away. Staring past Blake's fingers, she nodded as she saw a large dark body leap through the air and splash down again. 'Quite a large pod if the area of churning water is an indicator.' It had been a while since she'd last seen dolphins and they gave her the warm fuzzies. 'I hope they come closer.'

Continuing to the end of the wharf, they watched the show being put on out in the harbour. Leaning against the rail, Georgie couldn't stop smiling. A perfect start to their weekend in a wonderful location.

The dolphins eventually left and Blake had a light smile on his beautiful mouth as he watched the mammals. 'I remember dolphins swimming around the boat once when we were heading out to go fishing beyond the harbour entrance. I stopped the motor and we bobbed around for about twenty minutes watching them until they swam away.'

She turned and leaned back against the rail to look directly at him. Blake was good-looking in an outdoor kind of way. Tanned with beguiling eyes that didn't miss a thing as far as she was aware. Firm muscles from top to toe, fit without being excessive. Long legs that had her pulse thudding as she thought about them wound around hers.

'What's putting that look of surprise on

your face?' Blake asked. 'Have I got breakfast on my face?'

If only it was that simple. 'Yes,' she answered and laughed when he made to wipe his mouth. 'Easily fooled.'

Blake grabbed her and tipped her backwards so her upper body was leaning over the rail. Then he leaned over her and kissed her with a passion that made the thudding go crazy with need.

Georgie gripped his arms and kissed him back with all her longing pouring through to him.

'Wow.' Blake stepped back, pulling her upright. 'Talk about flicking a switch. Lights on in an instant.' His chest was rising and falling rapidly. He dropped his hands to his sides as he watched her. 'You're driving me to distraction, Georgie.'

'I know the feeling.' Was it wise to be this honest with him? For the first time ever she wanted to put out there how she felt, not to hide behind reasons for taking it slowly. They only had a week to go, and she didn't want to get to the end of it and not have given Blake some inkling to how she felt about getting closer.

'I believe you do.' He was still watching her, a serious glint in those grey eyes.

Blake took her hand. 'Come on. We're going on a picnic at the beach.' He began heading back down the wharf at a fast clip.

She hadn't been on a picnic since she was a kid. Hopefully this one would be a lot more fun. Maybe she would go swimming afterwards though. 'I can't wait.'

CHAPTER FIVE

EASY, MAN. TAKE this slowly.

There was a lot at stake; namely two hearts that could get battered beyond recognition if they weren't sensible. Blake accepted he and Georgie lived different lives in different parts of the country, lives he doubted either of them wanted to give up. They'd both worked so hard to get where they were; it wouldn't be easy to walk away and start over. But what if he fell hard for Georgie? Then what? Since catching up with this lovely woman who he was taking down to the beach for a prearranged picnic lunch, he had begun letting go some of the fear from the past. Just not quite enough to want to risk falling in love with her.

But he was getting ahead of himself.

They were starting a fling. That's what they had agreed to.

'Cat got your tongue?' Georgie asked as they stepped onto the sand at French Bay.

'Something like that.' Not a cat in sight, but one look at Georgie and his tongue was in a knot and his throat blocked with longing.

'Got it bad, mate.' Noah's words tripped into his head. Blake stumbled, straightened, his hands tightening on the cooler he was carrying filled with their lunch. Noah had always teased him relentlessly whenever he caught him watching his sister. Had he suspected there was more to his adoration of Georgie than a typical horny young guy lusting after a hot girl? He was never going to know, and he was glad. Falling for his best friend's sister would come with some hard reminders of his role in her life. Not that he'd be any different without Noah here to keep an eye on him, but he felt more relaxed without him. There was a first. Not wanting Noah in on something going on in his life.

'The water looks so tempting,' Georgie said as she placed her bag and the sun umbrella he'd brought along on the grassy edge of the beach. 'I'm going in.' With that, she was pulling her shirt over her head and tossing it on top of her bag, revealing her bikini-clad upper body. Then she was shaking her sexy butt out of her three-quarter pants before tossing them aside too.

The cooler hit the ground with a quiet thud as his fingers lost their grip on the handle. Georgie was curvy and desirable, her backside making his hands itch to cup each side. Her skin was evenly tanned and looked so soft. And when she swept her hair up on top of her head and tied it in place, her breasts rose to point upward, stealing his breath.

'Coming?' she asked with a grin.

'In a minute. I'll spread out the blanket and put the umbrella up first.'

Get my breath back, and my hormones under control before making a complete idiot of myself.

Nothing much had changed since those teenage years after all.

'So you brought your swimmers?' She was eyeing him up and down, the tip of her tongue at the corner of her mouth.

Sending his heart rate into overdrive. No calming down going on at all. 'These shorts are my swimmers.'

A frown appeared as she once again looked him up and down. 'Have you put sunscreen on?'

'Yes, Mum.' Should've said no and let those slim fingers do a number on his skin as she rubbed cream over him.

Another grin and she was off, racing down to the water like a girl let free for the day.

Blake watched her stepping into the sea, not wasting time feeling how warm it might be but taking long strides until it came up to those smooth thighs, then she dived under.

'Damn it.' Stabbing the umbrella pole into the ground at a useless angle, Blake stripped off his shirt, kicked out of his sneakers and took off after her.

Georgie was already swimming out towards deeper water, her strokes regular and strong.

He could match her and some. Within minutes he'd reached her and continued on, only stopping to tread water once he felt he was far enough from the beach to be alone with her. He caught her to him as soon as she came up beside him, wrapping his arms around her. 'Hey, Sunshine.'

Georgie wound her arms and legs around him, leaving him to keep them upright. 'Hey, yourself.' She planted a salty kiss on his mouth.

They bobbed up and down, further down as their kiss got deeper. Pulling his mouth free, Blake dragged in a lungful of air and said, 'I think we'd better move inshore a little so we can at least touch the bottom with our toes.'

Taking his hand, Georgie began dog paddling back the way they'd come until her feet were on the bottom. Then she caught him to her again and returned to kissing him as though she needed his air more than hers.

Under his palms her skin was warm yet cool, smooth and wet, sending shivers throughout his body. Those perky breasts held in place by the skimpy yellow bikini were pressed into his chest, while her legs were locked around his hips. His reaction was pure and simple. He wanted her. Now. He was so hard he ached, and throbbed.

'Georgie,' he groaned against her neck as he sucked her skin.

And groaned some more as her fingers tracked down his back to his butt. A firm squeeze by those fingers had his heart pounding, and the need for her threatening to burst out of him.

Sliding a hand between them he reached inside the miniscule pants covering her core, and slipped a finger inside where she was hot, and moist from more than the sea.

'Oh, yes. Don't stop,' Georgie groaned and took him in her hand to squeeze and rub him.

He couldn't have stopped if the beach had suddenly filled up with a busload of sightseers. Thankfully he'd chosen an empty beach for their lunch, one not on the tourist track. At least he hoped he'd got that right because right now there was no halting this need pounding through him.

'Blake,' she gasped. 'Yes, again. And again.'

He obliged, feeling her heat and the tightening as she orgasmed.

They slumped into each other, gasping for air as they held on to one another to stay upright as the light waves bumped them around on their toes. He felt Georgie begin to laugh before he heard her, and looked down into her sparkling eyes. 'You are so beautiful.' Especially when she was relaxed and her hair was spilling out of the restraint she'd had it in. The splashes of water on her face and the sated look in her eyes added to her attraction.

Her mouth split into a wide grin. 'You say the nicest things.'

'I meant it.'

The grin slipped a little as she stared at him. 'Thank you.'

She wasn't used to receiving compliments? Or maybe she didn't believe them. He'd have to give her some more. It wouldn't be hard. She was stunning, and so sexy.

'You've gone serious on me.' Georgie pulled back, disappointment wiping away that grin.

Hardly. Reaching over the gap he caught her to him, tucked her against his chest. 'You have no idea what was going through my mind, but trust me, it wasn't bad.'

Pulling her head away from him so she

could eyeball him, she said quietly, 'We just had the most amazing experience, didn't we?'

'It was sublime.' Leaning down, he kissed her. 'Next time will be even more so. Pulling back, he locked his eyes on her. Come on. Let's crack open the bottle of wine that's in the cooler.'

Her eyebrows rose. 'You really did prepare for this, didn't you?'

She didn't know the half of it yet. Once they'd agreed to come out to Akaroa he'd got busy looking up restaurants and accommodation, starting with the lunch in that cooler on the beach. 'Not for what we just did, but everything else, yes. A good start to the weekend.' He grinned, feeling so comfortable with Georgie it'd be scary if he thought about where they were headed. So he wouldn't. He'd make the most of every moment they shared and leave everything else until another day.

'*And* it was always going to be out of this world,' she added quietly.

So quietly he wondered if he'd heard correctly. It was what he was thinking so he might've been mistaken but he'd go with it.

It made him feel great. Taking her hand, he pulled them both inshore and up the beach.

Georgie flicked the blanket out on the sand and flopped down. 'I haven't spent a day at the beach like this in for ever.'

'How many times have you done that in the water?' he said with a laugh.

'Relax, that was a first.' She grinned.

He felt absurdly pleased. Opening the cooler he took out the wine, poured them each a drink. 'To the weekend,' he said as they tapped their glasses together. She didn't say a word, merely sipped the Chardonnay and gazed out over the beach as he reached into the cooler for the plates. 'Hope you still like crayfish?'

'You certainly know how to spoil a woman.' She was laughing softly as she watched him open up the containers of salad, crayfish and fresh bread rolls.

'It's not something I do very often, but I couldn't resist doing something special for today. Careful,' he said as he saved his wineglass from spilling over when she leaned close.

Her kiss was like a warm caress on his

chin, having missed his mouth because he'd moved so sharply.

He was quick to remedy that and shifted slightly so his lips covered hers. He could go on kissing her all afternoon and long into the night. She made his heart sing, and his body hot. With a long, deep breath, he pulled back, and tapped his finger lightly on her chin. 'Let's eat.'

Before I go crazy enough to take you right here on the beach.

Which would not be a good look when at any moment people could come walking around the corner. Some things were best kept between themselves.

Georgie stared down the beach to the glistening water and sipped her wine. If she was asked to get up and go for a walk or even a swim right now she'd have to refuse. Her muscles seemed to have lost their ability to function properly. Every part of her body felt soft and floppy, like wet tissue paper. Out in the water, when Blake touched her intimately, he'd woken her body up so that she'd been aware of every inch of it, while at the same time the sensations he created were off the scale.

Glancing sideways, she soaked up the sight of the long legs and flat abdomen and the wide chest sprawled beside her. He was gorgeous. More gorgeous than she'd imagined. His face was relaxed, his eyes hidden behind classy sunglasses, his hair all spikey curls now that it had dried with the salt stiffening it. Definitely gorgeous.

She shimmied down the blanket to stretch full length next to him. 'That was a superb lunch.' Crayfish was her absolute favourite seafood, something she only had occasionally, not wanting to lose the sense of pure indulgence she got when devouring it.

'You're welcome. Just hope you've got an appetite for dinner.' His hand covered her thigh, his fingers slowly caressing her skin.

'There's more?'

'Of everything,' he muttered.

Her heart filled, and she laughed. 'I can handle that.'

Blake rolled on to his side, put his head in the palm of his hand. 'You remember when you used to go out partying with your girl-friends on a Saturday night?'

'Sure can. We got up to all sorts of trouble.' They'd thought they were quite the thing back then, but in fact they hadn't been anything more than girls having fun without getting into any sort of trouble.

'Me and Noah, and some of our friends, used to watch you leaving for town and wish we could join you. You were hot, all of you, but for me, you in particular.'

'We always told you to go away.' Blake used to hang around trying to get her attention, but she hadn't realised he was quite that fired up about her. Probably just as well. She'd have thought that gross considering he was her little brother's mate. The four-year age gap was huge back then.

'You sure did.' He leaned in and kissed her. 'It's been a long wait, but worth it.'

Georgie snuggled into him and kissed him back. And kissed him some more, and took his kisses and held them close and lost all track of time and where they were. It didn't matter. She was in a bubble with only Blake and their kisses while their bodies touched each other's, and life was a dream.

The dream continued all afternoon. When they became too hot and wound up with longing, Blake packed up their gear and took her hand to walk back to the car, and drove them a short distance to a luxurious cottage on another beach where they were booked to stay the night. Within minutes of opening the doors and windows to let the light offshore breeze through they were falling onto the super-king-sized bed, stripping each of their clothes and touching one another all over.

Later Georgie spied a spa pool out on the deck which she quickly climbed into.

Blake brought out glasses of wine before joining her to soak away the tightness in his body. 'More exercise than I'm used to.' He grinned.

Good. Hate to think he'd been making out lots with some other woman, Georgie thought as she sipped her wine and shuffled deeper into the hot water. Ahh, the warmth. Even on a summer day it felt wonderful, relaxing her sore, out of practice muscles. 'I could stay here for ever.'

'You'd look like a prune.'

'Thanks, pal.' She changed the subject.

'Do you think you should give Sarah a ring? See how she's doing?' She'd hate for anything to happen and Blake not know about it straight away. That'd put the biggest dampener possible on their fun.

'What? And interrupt her and Dad snoozing together on that narrow hospital bed? Good idea.' He headed inside to get his phone. Ten minutes later he returned. 'All good. Andrew's even said Mum might be able to go home tomorrow. Her bloods are improving after the last transfusion. The white count has returned to normal so an infection's unlikely.'

'That is good news.'

'Yeah. It is.' Relief poured off him, then he tensed again. 'Now we only need a good outcome on the lab report.'

'You're looking for trouble.' She climbed out of the spa and wrapped a towel around herself before winding her arms around Blake, holding him tight. 'I know it's difficult, but Sarah is getting better. Hold on to that.'

He brushed a kiss across her forehead. 'I'm working on it.'

He needed a distraction, and she had the

perfect idea. Slipping her hand down the front of his shorts she covered his manhood and began softly rubbing up and down.

A sharp intake of breath told her this was working.

'Slow down, Georgie. I'm not doing this alone. You're joining me.' He scooped her up in his arms and headed for the bedroom.

Dinner at a French restaurant on the main street of the town was delicious. Walking back to the cottage hand in hand with Blake, Georgie couldn't imagine life getting any better. 'This is magic,' she told him. 'I can't remember ever having such a wonderful time.'

'It makes me think about what I might've been missing out on by staying away from everyone.' He squeezed her hand. 'We might've got to spend time together a lot earlier.'

She thought about that. 'I don't know. I haven't been ready to have a relationship, even a fling, since my marriage folded.'

'More hurt on top of the rest?'

There was even more he didn't know about. She spoke in a low monotone, trying to quell the sudden ache in her heart.

'I lost a baby. Tommy and I had tried for a while and just when it seemed I might never get pregnant, it happened. Then I lost it.'

Blake instantly wrapped her in his arms and held her tight. 'Oh, Georgie, that's awful. How did you cope?'

'I just got on with things,' she replied against his chest. 'And decided I won't ever go through that again.' Except it could be time to move forward, along with everything else. Easy said.'

'I can't begin to imagine what you must've gone through. It's one of my nightmares to lose someone close again, and yet you've been there, and survived.' His hug intensified. 'You never cease to amaze me with your fortitude.' His hand was stroking her hair down her back. 'I am lost for words.'

'There's nothing to say.'

Just keep holding me.

'You are so strong. So damned tough, you amaze me.' His hug tightened some more.

Pressed against him, she felt safe and cared about. She smiled softly.

And in the morning when Blake woke her before the sun had risen to suggest they go to the top of a nearby hill to acknowledge Noah's anniversary, she kissed him. 'I'll take some of those flowers that are in the vase on the table and scatter the petals over the grass.' Noah had loved the outdoors, spent a lot of time hiking in the hills and skiing the snowfields. Being on a hill this morning, watching the sun come up, was the closest she could be to him.

'He was the best friend anyone could ever wish for,' Blake said as they sat on the hilltop watching the sun make its appearance. 'I've never stopped missing him.'

Dribbling some petals from her hand, Georgie agreed. 'Me either. I'd even be happy for him to be here acting like a pain in the butt.'

Blake was quiet for a while, then, 'These past few days with you have helped me start letting go the pain and begin looking forward, to accept I can pursue my dreams of being happy and not fearing what can go wrong.'

Tears filled her eyes at his admission. Thirteen years was too long for Blake to have suffered so much. Too long for her too. They'd wasted their younger years, when they could've both been happy with partners, families, the whole works, instead of following their careers so intensely while ignoring what was required for a balanced life. 'I have too. We can't go back and retrieve what we've lost, but we can make the most of every day that's ahead.'

'You think?'

'I know.' She did, deep inside. Looking around them at the hills and the sea beyond, the township below, the flower petals on the grass beside her, Georgie felt more knots falling away. She was free to move on, to love and be happy. She didn't have to feel guilty for living, or afraid of any hurt that might come her way. She'd survived and could now move on with an open mind. Look for love. A sideways glance told her she was close to finding it with Blake. Or was she looking for something that wasn't there? That could so easily be the case. All sorts of hope and excitement had begun rushing in, filling her up with wonder. She needed to slow down. Or take things one step at a time, starting with supporting this man who'd weaved a

spell around her and made her start looking at the world differently.

'I like your confidence. I'll go with one
day at a time for now.'

'No problem.' She understood, and one
day was better than none at all. Turning,
she reached for him, slid her arms around
the body she'd come to know very well in
the past twenty-four hours. 'Blake, you are
wonderful.'

A stunned look appeared in those grey
eyes, and when he opened his mouth, she
covered it with hers, not wanting to hear
him say he wasn't interested in her other
than as a friend who'd become a lover. They
were having a fling, probably a very short
one since he was returning to Auckland in
a week, but she'd deal with that when he'd
left town if she had to, not now out here in
the fresh air with the hills around them and
her heart playing a merry tune in her chest.

Blake returned her kiss with a fervour
she had not known before. It was as though
he'd decided, like her, to make the most
of now and not waste time thinking about
anything else.

That suited her perfectly. Falling backwards, she sprawled across the grass, taking Blake with her.

Eventually they had to return to reality and life on the other side of Little River, and the time came round far too quickly. Georgie sighed as she reluctantly buckled her seatbelt for the return trip. 'I've had a fantastic time, thank you, Blake.'

Blake smiled. 'Thanks, Georgie. It was good up on the hill. That was the first time I've remembered Noah on the anniversary without getting angry at the injustice of life. Instead I recalled how much zest he had for the outdoors and the way he went about making sure he was always doing something to keep fit for the hikes he did. I owe that to you.'

'To us. Getting together has been good on so many levels. Noah's only one of them.' She almost giggled. Almost, before managing to act her age. 'I haven't had so much sex in for ever. I'm going to ache from head to toes for days.'

Blake threw her a wicked grin. 'That'll look good on my résumé should I rewrite it.'

Yeah. He was happy again. Which made her even happier. 'Now what sort of job would you be applying for with those credentials?'

'Wouldn't you like to know?' He laughed, then frowned as he stared at the van in front of them. 'Whoa. Watch out.'

'What's going on? Did I miss something?'

'That van swerved halfway over the white line. The driver must've been distracted for a moment. He seems to have it under control now.'

'That's dangerous around here.' They were on a windy road heading up the side of a hill now, and there wasn't a lot of margin for error. She tried to see into the van. 'Looks like there's a few people inside. Guess they're all talking, and it would be easy to lose focus briefly.'

'Not the way to drive—' Blake swore and braked sharply. 'What the—?'

Georgie stared in horror as the van veered towards the edge. It didn't stop, went over the side. 'Stop, Blake. Pull over.'

He was already parking on the verge a few metres beyond where the van had disappeared, flicking the hazard lights on as he scrambled out of the car.

Georgie leapt out, phone in hand, ready to press 111 for the emergency services if needed. At the edge of the road she stared down at carnage, her heart sinking. The van had rolled at least once before slamming into a tree which appeared to be the only thing saving it from going all the way to the bottom some hundred metres or more below. 'I'll call this in.'

'I'm going down.' Blake was already on his way.

After talking to the ambulance service, Georgie pocketed her phone and followed him, slipping and sliding on the steep slope.

Above them she heard other vehicles stopping. 'Hey, want a hand down there?' someone yelled out.

'Don't know what to expect yet,' Blake called back.

'I've called the emergency services,' Georgie said. 'But someone might want to get onto them. They'll want updates as we have them. Tell them there are two doctors here, and we'll likely need the rescue helicopter.' The hospital was more than an hour away by road.

'Female thrown out of the van.' Blake was peering in through a hole in the shattered windscreen. 'I can see three people inside. No, make that four. Hello? Can anyone hear me?'

'Don't you dare get inside before you've checked that the van can't move and roll down the hill,' Georgie said through gritted teeth. There was enough of a disaster here without adding to it. And the thought of Blake getting hurt was tying her stomach in knots.

'On to it.'

Georgie checked he was making sure the van was firmly wedged as she crossed to the woman lying in an awkward bundle like a rag doll on the grass. 'Hello? I'm Georgie, a doctor. Can you hear me?'

No response. Blood oozed from the woman's head, and her legs were at odd angles to the rest of her body. Georgie felt for a pulse. Throb, throb, throb. Phew. The woman wasn't out of trouble, but at least she was alive. No other major external bleeding apparent, and no sign of swelling in the ab-

domen area. The ribs didn't appear to have
been pushed inwards. She wouldn't move
the woman without fitting a neck brace in
case of a spinal injury.

There was nothing on hand to use for
a temporary swab for the bleeding head
wound. There were tissues in the car but
she wasn't about to climb back up there
when this woman needed her attention.
Hopefully someone else would turn up any
minute who might have a supply.

Georgie couldn't do much else until help
arrived, and Blake might need assistance
with the people inside the mangled vehicle.
Reluctant to step away from this woman,
she looked around to see if anyone else
had come down the hillside but no one was
about. She'd pop back every few minutes
to check on the woman.

At the van, she drew a breath. Blake was
squeezed inside the cramped space between
two women, working on one as though
nothing was out of order. Her heart softened for this man she already adored. 'Need
a hand? I don't want to leave the first patient
for long spells. She's got a GCS of four. Stat
two.' Time was critical to get her to hospital

where emergency doctors with all the equipment required could save her life.

'No one quite serious in here that I can see. But I could do with a hand to triage these people to make sure, then you can get back to her.' He didn't look up. 'The woman in front of you is twelve on the scale. She's in shock but seems physically unscathed. I haven't got to the men in the back yet.'

'I wonder if the driver had a medical event,' Georgie said aloud as she pulled her shoulders together to make herself small as possible to push through the narrow gap into the interior. 'Nothing to indicate cardiac failure.'

'Stroke? Aneurism?'

'Again, nothing to suggest so, but if it was a mild stroke, it's possible. Except she's unconscious, though that could be due to impact rather than whatever caused her to drive off the road.' The doorframe was firm against her shoulders and she tried swivelling a little to get through. 'How did you get through here?'

'With difficulty.'

Looking beyond the two women, Georgie

saw two men sprawled over the back seats. 'Hello, can either of you hear me?'

'I can,' one muttered. 'I'm stuck, can't get my foot out from under the seat in front of me.'

'Any other injuries?'

'Not that I can tell.'

'Right, we'll get to you shortly. What about your friend?'

'He's not saying anything, even when I shake him. There's a lot of blood.'

'Maybe lay off the shaking. We don't know what injuries he's got.' Georgie shuddered at the thought of fractures being shaken. 'I'll go back there,' she told Blake.

'No, I'll do that. You stay with these two where you can get out to go to the driver.'

He didn't want her taking a chance on being caught in the back if something went wrong and the van moved? Well, she didn't like the idea of Blake stuck back there either. But arguing only wasted precious time. These people needed their attention. 'Fine.'

Waiting while he awkwardly moved and slid through a gap by the seats and over into the back section, she focused on the woman by the door. 'I'm Georgie, a doctor. What's your name?'

'Evelyn.'

'Evelyn, can you move your legs?'

'I think so. It's going to hurt getting out through that narrow space though.'

'Hurt where?' Georgie asked.

'I don't know. My hip hurts and my neck.'

Blake looked over his shoulder. 'Whiplash is a possibility. I've checked her over and didn't find anything serious.'

Georgie focused on Evelyn. 'When they arrive we'll get the ambulance paramedics to put a neck brace on you, Evelyn. Now which hip hurts?'

'This one.' The woman tapped her right hip.

'Have you ever had problems with it before? A hip replacement? Arthritis?' The leg didn't look as though the hip had dislocated, but once Evelyn shifted that could change.

'Nothing.'

'When the van rolled do you remember any impact in that area?'

'Yes, I slammed into the side of the seat where the bar is.'

'Can you lift your leg for me?'

Evelyn did that, wincing with pain.

It probably wasn't fractured for her to be able to do that, but Georgie wasn't taking any chances. 'Right, you'll stay here until the fire service arrives.'

'No. I want out of here. It's creeping me out. What if the van moves, rolls further down the hill?'

Then we're all in trouble.

'It's firmly wrapped around the tree trunk. I don't think it's going anywhere.' Georgie mentally crossed her fingers. It had better not.

'What about Glenda? Is she going to be all right? She had a headache before we crashed.'

'She'll be the first to be taken to hospital when help arrives.'

'Want some help?' A man spoke from close by. 'I'm not a medic of any description but might be of some use.'

'Can you keep this woman company, talk to her, hold her hand if necessary? Her name's Evelyn. She wants to get out but that's not wise until we've got the paramedics and their gear to assist. She'll be bruised and possibly has hurt her neck,' Georgie answered as she turned around with difficulty to look at the other woman lying half on, half off her seat with the safety belt digging into her chest and stomach.

'No problem. Hi, my name's Murray and we're going to get you out of this mess.' He was already reaching for the woman's hand.

'Thank you.'

The second woman groaned, and lifted an arm before dropping it again, crying out as though struck by pain.

'Hey, I'm Georgie, a doctor. You've been in an accident. Can you hear me?'

The woman's eyes blinked open, shut.

'Good, now I'm going to touch your arms and legs looking for fractures. Can you blink if it hurts anywhere?'

Again the woman managed to open her eyes briefly, and this time she gave a slight nod. 'Arms.'

'Both arms?'

Blink.

'Right. I won't touch them.' Georgie ran her hands over the woman's thighs and knees but could go no further as her seat had been shoved close to the one in front.

They'd need cutting equipment to free her. 'Now, try a deep breath.'

A short gasp was all the woman could manage.

Georgie ran her hands over her chest and ribs as far as she could reach. There was a severe indent on the ribs at the left side. The woman's breathing was short but regular, suggesting her lung hadn't been punctured by a fractured rib. Stat two. Make it three with that rib issue.

A woman appeared at the door. 'I hear sirens. Can I do anything to help you? I have done first aid courses for work.'

It was hard deciding who to give her attention to, but she really needed to go check on the driver. 'I'd like you to take my place to keep an eye on this woman. She's aware of us, and answers questions by blinking. She's in lots of pain, and mustn't move at all. If anything at all changes get someone to tell me or Blake, the guy in the back. He's another doctor.'

'No problem.'

Georgie squeezed her way back out of the van and crossed to her first patient to kneel down and take her pulse. 'Hello, can you hear me?' Still no response. She lifted an eyelid, got a blank stare. The pulse rate hadn't changed.

'What can we do?' More people were making their way down the slope.

'Apart from other medical people, keep everyone up on the road. There's not a lot of flat space and we don't need it taken up by hangers-on.' Georgie was torn between remaining with this woman and getting back to the seriously injured one in the van. She looked over the woman's body, felt around her ribs and over her abdomen again and found no changes. Her breathing had become erratic, short gasps in between stillness. An aneurism was looking more and more likely. The bleeding from the head wound had slowed to a trickle. They needed splints for those legs but she'd have to be patient.

'Excuse me, when you've got a moment the other doctor wants you in the van,' someone told her.

'On my way. Can you stay with this woman, and let me know instantly if she opens her eyes or tries to move?'

Back at the van, the man who was with

the woman nearest the door said, 'Evelyn says the woman on the grass is called Annie and she had a sudden massive headache just before the crash.'

'That ties in with what I'm thinking. Thanks for that.' Georgie again squeezed inside and found Blake still with the men in the back. 'What have we got there?'

'Internal bleeding caused by that seat arm that must've come free in the impact.'

'Is he still unconscious?'

'Yes, seems he hit the head rest on the seat in front as well.' Blake glanced back at her. 'I don't know how we're going to get these people out.'

'The fire brigade will have the jaws of life. Makes everything so much easier. I'm going to check this woman and get back to the driver.'

'How's she doing?'

'Looking more like an aneurism. Need that chopper here ASAP.'

'I think I can hear one,' said the man sitting with Evelyn. 'And paramedics are coming down the hill from the road.'

Relief filtered through Georgie. While

she and Blake knew what they were doing, the paramedics were highly trained and did this every day. 'I'll talk to them.'

Within fifteen minutes the driver of the van had been carried on a stretcher up the hill to be loaded onto the rescue helicopter while firemen were cutting the van open so the other men and women could be retrieved. The second seriously injured woman was also put on board the chopper and then the air was flattening everything around them as the rotors began spinning.

As the helicopter lifted off the road, Blake joined Georgie. 'Let's leave the paramedics to finish up. They've got the gear and the ambulances to take everyone back to hospital. It's all under control.'

Georgie briefly leaned against Blake and drew a deep breath. 'What a mess that van ended up in. It must've been terrifying for everyone sitting inside completely helpless as it plunged off the road.'

He hugged her to him. 'Very scary. I'm glad we saw it happen or who knows how long it might've been before someone found them.'

She hadn't thought of that. A shiver tripped down her spine. 'We were joined quite quickly so someone else must've seen it. But the consequences could've been terrible for the driver. Not that she's in the clear by a long way.'

Blake hugged her tighter. 'Once a doctor, always a doctor, eh?'

'Yeah,' she sighed. 'There's no such thing as taking time out, is there?'

'You wouldn't change a thing.' Blake took her hand. 'And what's more, we did it together.'

A warm feeling spread through her. 'Yes, we did.' It was kind of lovely to think they'd done that without thought or conflict, just go on with what had to be done and accepted each other's role.

'Come on. We've got a hill to clamber up.'

Now that the victims of the accident were on their way to hospital Georgie had relaxed and her legs were like jelly. The slope in front of them seemed to grow as she stared at it. 'One step at a time.'

A bit like how she was facing her new relationship with Blake. One step—or kiss—

at a time. And it couldn't be better. She hadn't felt this excited about anything in a long time. No matter how things unfolded in the future, she was making the most of today.

CHAPTER SIX

BLAKE SAT ON the back deck of his parents'
home, enjoying the sun while he ate breakfast, listening to the sound of tuis and bell-
birds as they flew from tree to tree and
fought for their patches. As soon as he'd
finished up here he'd head into the hospital
to spend time with his mother. Hopefully
she was feeling better today. The infection
that set in on Sunday and quickly gone rampant had at last been brought under control,
and leaving her even more exhausted, but
it was her lethargy that had them all worrying. She seemed to have lost the fight in
her. It had been a long week.

The shrill tone of his phone broke into
his thoughts. 'Morning, Mum.'

'Blake,' she was almost squealing. 'I
haven't got cancer. It's true. Andrew's been

in and he talked to Alastair while he was here. I'm in the clear.'

'Really and truly?' Blake slumped in the chair. 'Thank goodness for that.' He rubbed his face but the tears kept spilling down his cheeks. The biggest hurdle was over. Mum was going to be all right.

'I am in the clear,' she repeated as though she didn't believe it. But then, it was a lot to absorb suddenly, after the weeks of waiting and fearing the result. 'I'm okay,' she reiterated.

Okay didn't begin to describe the rush of relief pouring through him. Everything was going to be great. 'I'll be in soon.' He leapt up and stepped off the deck, looking around the back garden where he'd done some work over the days, trying to still the many worries tumbling around his head. His mother and her health. The latest problems with the infection that had taken hold. Georgie and their fling. Georgie's ability to ground him and make him want to look forward, not back. Georgie and that hot body that had him hard in a blink. Georgie had got under his skin and he didn't know how to move on. Or if he even wanted to. How was he going to leave Christchurch after this emotional roller-coaster ride? Easy, he had to. There was a job he had to return to. A position he'd worked hard for and wouldn't give up easily.

He had to tell Georgie his mother's news. Now. She was at work, helping another woman, another family, through a medical crisis so no doubt his call would go to voice mail. Didn't matter. He had to try. Hearing her voice always set him up for the rest of the day. 'Hey, Blake. You caught me at a good time. Much needed coffee in hand. What's up?'

He didn't need coffee to set his heart rate going fast, just Georgie. 'Mum hasn't got cancer.'

'Fantastic. Wow, what a relief. You've made my day. That's brilliant. Give her a hug from me, will you?' Georgie laughed. 'I know, I'm babbling, but it's been a bit of a strain waiting. Wish I could hug *you* right now.'

Blake felt his heart give way a little more. 'Cyber hugs coming your way. Want to do dinner tonight?'

'I've got a better idea. Why don't we spend the weekend together at my house?'

'What time will you be home? I'll be waiting on the deck.'

'Thank goodness you said yes. I suddenly wondered if I was being a bit too rash.' She was laughing softly. 'This is crazy, and I'm loving it. There's a key to the back door in the garden shed, under the seedling packets.'

He laughed too. It was so easy to do with this woman. 'I'm not good enough for the front door?'

'Next week, maybe. Oh, got to go. I'm needed in ED.' She hesitated. 'Take care.' Had she been going to say something else? Something more intense? Special?

Not likely. Too soon, if at all. They'd spent every spare moment together throughout the week since Akaroa, dining, making love, talking about the past, the present and not at all about the future, and that was fine. They were having a fling, and what a fling it was. But crunch time was coming. When the infection broke out and everyone saw how debilitating it was for his mother, he knew she wouldn't be getting back on her feet for quite a while so he'd organised almost another fortnight off work to support his family and help out around the house.

He had to be back in Auckland for a board meeting by Friday week. Not attending would not be tolerated by the senior partners. By then he'll have been away nearly four weeks. He was still getting his head around that, since he didn't do staying so long with those that mattered for fear of getting so involved he couldn't walk away. At least with having his own house and the job he'd worked so hard to obtain, he knew he had to go home. He couldn't stay here any longer. Especially not so he could continue having a fling. He'd laugh if that didn't hurt. What had he done? Georgie was so special, and she'd got through his barriers so damned easily it had him wondering if he'd been trying to keep her out at all.

Slipping the phone into his back pocket, he began pulling the dead sweetcorn plants out of the ground. The plants came out easily and he put them in the compost bin before getting the fork from the garden shed to turn the soil over, picking out the weeds as he went. The rhythm of pushing the fork in, lifting it laden with soil, turning it and dropping the soil back to poke and break apart the clods quietened him. Soon memories of playing on the lawn with his sisters, kicking a football with his dad, hearing stories from his mother as she planted bulbs, came flooding back. He'd had a great childhood. Secure, loved and shown how to work for what he wanted. From things they'd said, his sisters and their husbands did the same with their kids. What was that like? By staying away, he'd missed out on many celebrations and fun times together with them all.

Glancing around the yard, he could picture himself playing with a toddler. Hell, he could see himself pushing a child on the swing that now stood in the corner. Not anyone's child but his. Laughter and shrieks of excitement would fill the air. Or a baby crying, waiting to be fed. His heart would beat hard. His heart *was* beating hard.

He stabbed the ground with the fork. There wasn't a baby or any children to interfere with any decisions he and Georgie made. Nor was there likely to be. He'd used protection every time. It was an unbreakable rule. He had never had unprotected sex. Chances were Georgie wouldn't want to risk getting pregnant either. She would not want to go through the pain of losing another baby. Or even just the worry of that happening throughout a pregnancy. The beating in his heart slowed. Damn. He should be saying thank goodness, because he'd sworn he'd never be a parent.

Stab, stab, went the fork. He had never had this conversation with himself before. There'd been no reason because he understood exactly where he stood on the subject of parenthood. It would not happen. But he had been thinking about the future and Georgie in the same sentence. It had to be because their relationship had taken off in such a hurry and he was still getting his head around it. They were happy together. It was nothing like when they'd been young and annoying the hell out of each other. This was different. Comfortable. Understanding. Caring. And he loved it. That didn't mean he loved Georgie. No, he didn't. So why this feeling that he mightn't be able to live without her? Wasn't that love? Slow down. He was getting ahead of himself. Too

many emotions were ramping through him
since his mother's call. Too fast, too soon.

He would be heading home to Auckland
soon. That was a solid fact. No changing it.

Tonight he was going to stay with Georgie, in her space, and relax. Everything
was looking up for his mum, and now he
and Georgie could have some fun without
having to pause and take a breath as they
waited for the results that would banish the
pall hanging over his family.

Georgie looked at her watch for the ump-
teenth time in the last hour. Four thirty-five.
What was making the time drag so slowly?
Apart from the fact her last patient for the
day was late for her consultation, and she
was sitting here twiddling her thumbs when
she could be using the time to look for any
incoming results on yesterday's patients'
lab tests? Blake, of course. She wanted to
get home and sit down with him, to chat
about their days, and Sarah's wonderful
news, to share some wine and make dinner.

Patients at the private and public hospitals were awaiting her visit once she'd finished here at Scott's Women's Health. It

would be hours before she got home and could spend time with Blake. Hours and hours. Georgie laughed at herself. About two, maybe two and a half. Not exactly a lot. Would she be this harebrained when he returned to Auckland and she wasn't seeing him at all? Daily phone calls weren't going to cut it. They'd remind her of what she was missing out on. Making love, sharing a meal, walking along the Avon. A hundred little things that were her and Blake together. This was more than a fling. For her anyway. She'd fallen for him hard and fast, and suddenly couldn't imagine life without Blake in it every single day.

'Georgie, Sonia Davis is here to see you.' Jane, the receptionist, led a young woman into the room.

'Hello, Sonia.' Georgie held her hand out. 'I'm Georgie Price. Please, take a seat.'

'Hello, Doctor. I'm sorry I'm late but I got a flat tyre on the way.' The woman did look a little dishevelled.

'That's fine.' She closed the door behind Jane and returned to her desk. 'You've been referred by your GP as you've got endometriosis. Correct?'

'That's right. I'm ready to have a hysterectomy now that I've had my second baby.'

Where was the husband? Or partner? Georgie knew this was hard enough for any woman to be going through without having to do it on her own. 'You've had counselling for what's ahead? You and your partner?'

'We have. Dave would like to be here but he's in Dunedin for work and couldn't change his roster. Mum's looking after the kids.' Sonia looked crestfallen.

'That is a shame. However, let me examine you and then we'll go through the procedure. I'll send in a booking for Theatre and we'll have an answer by tomorrow and hopefully your family will be able to arrange things to suit so you have support at the time of your surgery.'

Relief blinked out from Sonia's face. 'Thank you so much. Dave is planning on taking leave and has warned his bosses that it could be any time in the next few weeks. I really wanted him here today to be able to ask you questions, but he couldn't avoid going south.'

'It's always better if you can bring someone with you. Two sets of ears are more reliable than one. If you have any worries after today's appointment please call the office and they'll get a message to me and I'll get back to you.' Georgie stood up. 'Right, can you sit in the gynae chair and I'll take a look?'

When Sonia left fifteen minutes later, Georgie headed out to her car to drive to the public hospital to do a round of her patients there. By the time she reached home it was nearly seven and she was humming inside and out. Blake was staying with her for the weekend. Woo hoo.

Disappointment rose fast when she realised Blake wasn't waiting on the deck for her to arrive. Nor was he inside.

Relax. He'll turn up.

He was reliable.

At least she had time to take a shower and change into something casual. Pouring a wine, she took a sip. It was a bit sour. The bottle was one she'd opened earlier in the week and it had been oaky then. She took another sip and it was fine. What was that about?

When she came out of the bathroom the

smell of something delicious reached her. She grinned. Blake was here. Sauntering into the kitchen, she said, 'I hope that's dinner I can smell.'

'It'll go cold if you don't put on something more than that towel.' He reached for her. 'Though you do look wonderful.' His mouth covered hers and for a few minutes she was aware of nothing but Blake.

When they broke apart both were breathing heavily. She locked eyes on him.

And he laughed. 'To hell with dinner.'

Taking his hand, she led him down to her bedroom, letting the towel fall to the floor on the way. This was going to be the weekend of her life.

The weekend became a week, followed by the next weekend. They spent hours making love in bed, on the couch and in other places she'd never tried before. 'I'm surprised I can walk at all,' Georgie said one night as they snuck back inside from the deck. 'I think every bone in my body, every muscle, has been having a workout.' She grinned.

'Here, this'll help.' Blake handed her a frosted glass of wine.

She sipped the wine, and shuddered.

'That tastes a bit off.' Like the night Blake moved in temporarily. Since then she hadn't noticed anything different about the wine she liked but now that slightly sour taste was back. 'Maybe I'll have a sparkling water instead.'

Blake took her glass and tasted it. 'Seems all right to me.' He shrugged and headed out to the deck, her glass in his hand. 'I'll put some steaks on the barbecue.'

The deck was used for so many things these days the rest of the house apart from the bedroom and bathroom were almost obsolete. Until Blake headed back to Auckland.

She tried not to think about him leaving, but as the days sped past, it was getting harder to deny their fling was running fast towards the finish line.

Her heart slowed. Blake was going back to Auckland. Only a few days left to make the most of him. She was going to miss him so much it was hard to comprehend. Impossible to think about not seeing him regularly, to have him close by and be able to unwind with after a difficult day at work. What were they going to do? Go their separate ways with Blake visiting when he came home on those rare occasions he did come to see his parents? Or would she spend her weekends flying up to Auckland to be with him? 'Blake—' She paused.

'Yes?'

She wanted to know so much. Not now. They still had days ahead to make love, laugh and talk, share space and time. 'Want a salad with that steak?'

'It's in the fridge.'

I love him.

The bottle of water slid from her fingers. Picking it up, she filled a glass with the bubbly water. Somehow, without any effort, she'd fallen in love with Blake Newman. Funny how she'd never thought she'd fall in love so quickly. After her first relationship fiasco, she'd always believed she'd go slowly and make sure she got everything right next time. It didn't work, hence her failed marriage. Went to show how wrong she could be. There'd been nothing slow about falling for Blake, no checking out where he stood in this. Chances were that he'd be telling her *'thanks for everything but nothing's changed, see you next time I come to town'* and then he'd walk out the door, closing it behind him.

She had to work out what to do about it. First find out where she stood with him, if he felt anything more than friendship with benefits for her, or if she was wasting her time and giving her heart a battering it certainly didn't need. But not tonight. Tonight was for enjoying. So was the weekend. Maybe on Monday she'd talk to him. Possibly on Tuesday. When had she become so gutless? That happened the moment she realised Blake meant a lot more than a friend to her, meant more than a short-term lover. Like right about now.

Not the way to go, Georgie-girl. You've got this far in life by being strong.

Strong meant hiding behind her parents, using them as her excuse to stay in Christchurch? Using Noah's death as the reason not to get close to anybody?

'You okay?' Blake's voice sounded full of concern as he stood on the other side of the counter watching her.

Wouldn't he love to know what was tearing through her mind? 'All good.'

'Really?'

'Really.' She was, if she closed down her brain and went with the flow. Opening drawers she got plates and cutlery, then salad servers to take out to the table on the deck. The table where they'd made love. How her life had changed in the past couple of weeks. For the better. 'Here, take these. I'll get the salad and dressings.'

He was still watching her far too carefully for comfort.

Brushing her lips over his chin and shivering at the hot sensations that light stubble gave her, she smiled from deep inside. 'Just daydreaming about what we've been getting up to.' Despite all the worries about what lay ahead, she was happy. They were great together in so many ways.

Instead of taking the plates and cutlery, Blake caught her chin in his palm. His forefinger caressed her mouth. 'Why daydream when we've got the real thing right here?'

'Because I'm greedy and want it all.'

His eyes widened at that. He took a step back, not breaking the eye contact.

Georgie went very still, which only underlined what she'd said, even when she hadn't meant to put it out there. Not like that. Certainly not now. 'We're getting on so well I can't imagine it coming to an end. When you're not right beside me, I bring up the images of being with you in all ways possible.'

Reaching for the plates, Blake gave her a wry smile. 'I'd better get back to the steak.'

'Blake, I'm not trying to put pressure on you. Or me for that matter. Being with you, having this fling, is so wonderful I have to pinch myself at times to make sure it's real.' She would not think how she was going to cope once Blake left. Going back to normal, spending time with friends, her parents, at home with a good book, taking walks in Hagley Park seemed dull as dull could get. Yet she'd been happy with that until Blake turned up in her life, and now the idea of returning to that was as exciting as eating porridge without cream and brown sugar.

'It's real all right.' His grin backed his words, before he headed back out to the deck where the sound of meat sizzling on the hot plate tempted her to follow.

She smiled to herself. There were still plenty of days for a lot more lovemaking.

A whole weekend with no babies due, no rostered duties, lay ahead. A weekend to spend with Blake. She was going to grab it with both hands and make the most of everything that came her way. Blake was the best thing to ever happen to her.

Friday night floated into Saturday morning and shopping at Riccarton Mall.

'Something else we have in common,' Blake grunted as he stacked bags of clothes in the back of Georgie's car.

'Come on. I only shop once a season.' There'd been a definite nip in the air when they'd managed to climb out of bed that morning. 'Autumn's just around the corner and I don't want to get caught out.'

'You mean in those two full wardrobes you've got, there aren't any clothes suitable for the next season?' Blake was laughing as he closed the door.

'We are two peas in a pod, aren't we?'

'Nothing to do with peas. But yes, I own up. I have suits from here to Africa but they're my uniform for work.'

'You wear a different one every day of

the month? And change your shirts at lunch and dinnertime?' He'd just bought six shirts.

'I give away a lot to the charity shops.'

She laughed. 'That makes it all right then.' Something she could do as well. Her wardrobes were so full it was a struggle to go through and find what she wanted to wear. Clothes were her thing, though she tended to keep to understated outfits for work so didn't have a lot of fancy dresses and blouses because there weren't lots of occasions for getting dressed up. Or hadn't been until Blake turned up. And now that she'd started wearing more up-to-date clothes she wasn't going to stop when he left. Another notch in the zip had closed. She was getting her old self back, and enjoying it.

'What's next? Coffee? Lunch?'

'How about we drive over to Lyttleton for lunch. I hear there's a great bar-cum-café overlooking the harbour.'

'Can I drive?'

'Thought you didn't like having your knees up around your ears.' She tossed him the keys. It wasn't often she got to be the passenger and she liked it. As though she was being pampered somehow.

As he set the seat further back, Blake said, 'I don't understand why you've got a small car. Stylish, sure, got some power, yes, but there's no space.'

'It's economic, gets into most parking spaces and goes like a racing car when I want it to.' Fast driving wasn't her thing, but sometimes it felt good to go as fast as was legal on the motorway.

'I'm just about sitting on the back seat,' he said with a laugh.

'Get a move on or the bar will be closed by the time we arrive.'

'Yes, ma'am.'

Saturday ended with lovemaking in the shower and mugs of tea in bed afterwards. 'Like two oldies,' Blake joked as he drank from his mug.

'Nice and snug,' Georgie agreed.

Sunday was more of the same, and then Georgie went back to work on Monday feeling like a teen on a high. Or what she thought that might feel like. Blake was wonderful, everything she'd dreamed of a man being, back in the days when she used to dream about those things. Yes, when she'd been young and carefree.

Slamming her car door shut, she did a little dance on the spot, then looked around to make sure no one had seen her. Carefree. That was the word for how she felt. Not a worry in the world. Except that wasn't true. She was playing the avoidance game very well, if she believed that. Blake was leaving. Soon he'd be gone. Not out of her life for ever. That wasn't possible after this fling. They were making memories as vivid and sharp as any she'd known. But memories weren't going to be enough. She wanted the real deal—for ever.

They needed to talk. To let each other know what they were really feeling and thinking, regardless of how scary it might be to open up. Most of all, Georgie sighed, they needed time and it was running out.

Time was something she'd had a lot of over the years since her marriage failed. She'd filled it hiding from the past, and denying the future could be exciting and loving and, well, full of all the things she'd like to be happy. Now the need to get cracking with living at the top of the rainbow, enjoying everything that came her way, making the most of opportunities that presented, of loving with her whole heart, was taking over. All of that had to include Blake. So she had to talk to him. Before he left tomorrow. He'd had to bring his flight forward because of a board meeting he was obliged to attend. Which underlined the problems that lay ahead.

She strode inside Scott's Women's Health clinic and picked up the pile of notes in her file basket. 'Morning, everyone.'

'Hi, Georgie. You look like you've had a great weekend,' Jane said.

'I did. A fantastic one.'

'New blouse and skirt?'

'Yes. You like?'

'I do. Andrew wants to see you.'

She wondered what he wanted. 'On my way.'

Her phone vibrated. Blake.

Have a great day. xxx

You too. xxxx

I'm cooking tonight. xxxxx

Smiling, Georgie headed for the office next to hers. 'Morning, Andrew.'

'You're looking perky this morning,' Andrew said as he got up and went to close the door.

This had to be serious then. He was one of the senior partners in the practice so he had her full attention. She sat in the chair he indicated, and waited.

As he crossed to sit down on the nearest chair, he smoothed his trousers and pulled his shoulders back. Definitely a serious meeting. A bolt of concern hit her. Had she made an error with a patient? But surely she'd be the first to know? She thought back over the past weeks. But nothing raised any flags. So what else? It had to be important if that board-meeting look on Andrew's face was anything to go by. Her palms moistened, while her mouth dried.

'What's up?' The question came out too sharp, but she couldn't take it back.

'Relax, Georgie. Everything's fine.' Then why did he sound as though he was about to deliver a grenade with the pin already pulled?

'I hope so.' Ouch. That sounded weak,

something she wasn't around here. Or never showed anyway, not even to this man, who'd been behind her all the way since she'd first started training to become a gynaecologist and obstetrician under his tutelage. But he'd known her weaknesses, especially how she had to succeed no matter what. He'd even tried to tell her to take time out, become more rounded as a person, not so focused on her career, or she might burn out one day. So far he'd got that wrong.

'Right, let me put this out there. Tom has decided to start his retirement next month.' Andrew paused. 'And you are top of the list to replace him as a senior partner.'

What? 'Really?' This was a dream come true. From the moment she'd started working here she'd been dreaming of a senior partnership. The first step as a junior had been wonderful, but this was over the top exciting.

'Yes, really.' Andrew smiled. 'We had a breakfast meeting earlier this morning and everyone's in agreement. You are ideal for the position.'

Deep breath. Give the man an answer. She didn't have to waste time thinking about it. 'Thank you so much. It's unbelievable, really.'

Andrew came around his desk and held out his hand to shake hers. 'Congratulations. You deserve it.'

Shaking his hand, she knew she was grinning stupidly, but hey, she'd been aiming for this for so long. 'Thank you so much.' How exciting. Blake. She couldn't wait to tell him. He'd be thrilled for her. Wouldn't he?

I want this. More than anything.

A knot formed in her stomach. Now that she'd had a glimpse of what she could have with Blake if only she could let go of the stranglehold on her emotions, was it still the most important thing in her life right now? Hell, yes.

She went back to her office in a daze, her feet almost skipping. Senior partner. Woo hoo. How cool was that?

She wrapped her arms around herself, grinning. Senior partnership. She had to tell someone. Blake. She picked up the phone.

'Hey, have I got some news. I've been offered a senior partnership.'

'That's awesome. Georgie, I'm so proud

of you,' he said. 'Seriously proud. You must be stoked.'

'I keep pinching myself. It's still sinking in. Definitely have to celebrate tonight.'

'I reckon. I'm buying the champagne.'

There was a knock, and the receptionist put her head around the door.

'I've got to go. Talk later.' And share some delicious kisses.

CHAPTER SEVEN

LATE THAT AFTERNOON Blake stood on the back porch of his parents' nineteen-twenties house and watched his nieces and nephews running around like crazed monkeys.

So Georgie had been offered a senior partnership. Good for her. She deserved it. And did she sound thrilled, or what? Something he understood. The day he'd been offered his position at the orthopaedic practice he'd been ecstatic. He'd be even more so if, no, when, he was offered a senior partnership. It was the penultimate position in their careers. Georgie had now achieved it. This definitely called for a celebration tonight.

'Aren't those rascals cute?' his mother said from her seat beside him. She still looked tired but since coming home she'd begun to get some colour back in her complexion and be able to move around comfortably.

'They won't be when they finally crash. Bedlam will rule.' There was a smile in his heart for the little guys. Something about them got to him without any thought or care. He loved them, end of. It had been great catching up with his sisters and their families. Every hour was indelibly etched in his heart, ready to be taken back to Auckland when he headed away tomorrow. 'I don't get to see them often enough.' The moment the words left his mouth he knew he'd made a mistake.

Sure enough, his mother picked up on it straight away. 'You can always move back here.'

But was he ready to up stakes and shift his whole life back here? Tomorrow he'd go back to his real life: sterile, quiet and work filled. Yet Georgie was squeezing his heart. Her smiles, her understanding, her lovemaking. Damn it, everything about her had touched him beyond measure. What had started out as a fling which was meant to help put the past well and truly behind both of them had become something far more serious and brought the future into focus.

He had to face up to the fact he might be falling for Georgie whether he wanted to or not, in a way he hadn't done before with any woman. Other women had been easy to keep at the friends with benefits level. Georgie was not.

Then there was today's news. She'd been given an offer she wouldn't hesitate to accept. He couldn't blame her for that. So relinquishing the partnership she was so proud of was not going to happen. He couldn't ask that of her. That'd be beyond selfish. So back to square one. He lived in Auckland, she was staying in Christchurch. If anyone made the move, it had to be him, and he wasn't sure he could manage that. What if he came down here and they couldn't make it work? Whichever way, one of them would have to make huge sacrifices if they were to get together.

Blake swore under his breath. New Zealand wasn't exactly a big country. It took less than an hour and a half to fly between the two cities. They could be in either place for any party, dinner or family get-together with little trouble. It wasn't as though they'd be living on the opposite side of the world from the people who mattered the most to either of them. They could see how it went before making those changes required if they lived together. Except that was hardly a full-on commitment, and he'd want that if he was going to step up. So would Georgie. What's more, she deserved no less.

What did Georgie think about this? Would she say, *'Hey, it's been a great few days, but it's over and now we get back to normal'*? Remind him he hadn't been in a hurry for more than a fling? Somehow he doubted it. She'd said how being together had made her feel so happy and at ease over a relationship for the first time in years. He wanted to share that with her, help dispel any fear she had going forward. Commitment meant opening up to anything and everything.

Something he understood all too well, and had been avoiding for too long. Now, with Georgie, he felt he could put all that out there and not have to feel exposed. She wouldn't take advantage of his pain. Pain which was getting smaller the more time he spent with Georgie. They understood each other, knew what the other had been through. He was ready to move on for the first time since the night Noah died. Almost ready. All because she got him.

But did that mean they were together about everything? Nothing got any easier. Of course he could be looking for trouble when the answers might be straightforward.

He sent her a message. Another new habit, this keeping touch over trivia.

What time do you think you'll get away? Was looking forward to an evening together?

Blake smiled to himself. Of course not, but downplaying it was his way of dealing with emotions.

Any time soon.

Blake popped the cork and poured two glasses of champagne. Handing one to Georgie, he leaned in to kiss her. 'To you, you amazing woman. Congratulations on your promotion.'

She tapped their glasses together, her eyes shining with glee. 'It's pretty exciting.' She took a small sip, and leaned her hip against the counter, one foot tapping nonstop on the tiles. 'Actually, it's so unbelievable I have to keep pinching myself.'

'You're looking more like the Georgie I used to know. Can't keep your feet still or the smile from your face.' Next she'd be dancing around the room.

She moved and a big kiss landed on his cheek. 'Since you came to town my life has been changing in all directions.' Laughter burst from her as she locked those sparkling blue eyes on him. 'The most wonderful fling with a man I can't believe understands me better than I do myself sometimes. And he's so sexy as well. Then today's bombshell.' She grinned and swallowed some of her wine. 'Cheers to us.'

Tapping his glass against hers again, he took a mouthful. 'Cheers.' To them. To them and whatever lay ahead.

She drew a breath, and said in a quieter voice, 'Blake, these weeks have been the best of my life. The very best.'

'Culminating in this news,' he said quietly. It was epic, and yet it had raised questions about what they were going to do after he left Christchurch. He didn't want to finish what they had going, but even he understood it couldn't continue. It was the line between two futures and he wasn't sure he could give up everything to take a risk on his heart, and Georgie's.

'You go home tomorrow, back to your career. I've stepped up a rung with mine. I can't see how we can continue a fling and be happy about it. Tripping up and down the country for a night or two together?' She shook her head. 'I don't think I can do that. I'm an all or nothing kind of woman. Mostly nothing.'

Did she mutter, 'Until now'? His heart sank. He couldn't imagine not being a part of her life. So he was prepared to drop everything and move back here? His throat closed. Just like that? Give up everything he'd worked so hard for? Why not? Because he was afraid. Because he didn't trust himself to be able to let go the past completely. Clearing his throat, he said, 'Georgie, I worry that if we were to take this further the past might get in the way and ruin everything.'

'So am I,' she whispered. 'I want to think

I can handle whatever happens between us, can take the knocks. I want more, yet I can't ask you to give up what's important to you.'

'Georgie—' He needed time to think this through. She was everything to him—if he had the guts to step up and put his hand out. But could he do that and not look back in a few months' time and think he'd made a mistake? He was in love with Georgie, but did he *love* her? As in every way possible? Risk his heart? She'd look after it. But caution was such a habit. He didn't know what he wanted. Or wasn't ready to accept. Be honest. It was the only way to go. Placing a hand on her cheek, he said softly, 'I don't think either of us is ready for more than what we've had. We need time to be certain about the next step.'

The colour leeched out of her cheeks, and she straightened up. 'Sure you're not running away again?' When she wanted to hurt, seemed she went for the jugular.

Pain struck him in the chest hard. He was in love with this woman. Probably did *love* her. Yes, he was ready to admit that much.

So tell her and get down on your damned knees and beg her forgiveness, tell her how you feel and what you hope will unfold between you.

She sank onto a stool and took a big mouthful of wine. 'I'm sorry. I was out of order, saying that. You're right, we'd both have some major decisions to make.'

'We do.' Could be he *was* running away *again*. He was afraid to step up and take whatever hit him on the chin. Afraid to take a chance on not being hurt, of losing one of the people he gave his heart to. Suddenly Auckland seemed safe. A lot safer than remaining here and committing to Georgie. Better to let her down now than hurt her badly further down the track if their relationship didn't work out. A resounding 'no' slammed through his mind. No. He was not running away. He had to put Georgie before his own needs. But how when his heart was involved?

'I don't want to continue with our fling, only to have it dwindle away to nothing. I say it's over.' Georgie's fingers were rubbing her thighs hard. Her smile was wobbly, but her eyes were full of what looked like love to him.

His ribs were aching from the thumping

they were getting. This was really it? He didn't want that, nor was he ready to leap in and say he loved her, only to realise he'd got it wrong and hurt her. 'Catching up with you hasn't been what I'd ever have imagined, but I've no regrets whatsoever.' Another squeeze to his heart. Really? When she was his moon and his sun? How was he going to leave her behind tomorrow? He had to. He could not hurt her any more. Going home would give him the space to really take a long hard look at himself, and what he was going to do.

'Honest to the core. But I wouldn't like it any other way.' She straightened. 'It's been one heck of a day, and I'm shattered. Think I'll make a mug of tea and curl up in bed.'

The other night they'd sat up together in her bed, drinking tea and laughing over how they were like a couple of oldies. Now they were on a knife edge, their futures hanging in the balance.

He itched to reach for her, to haul her into his arms for one last time, but that would add to the pain bubbling up through his chest, spreading throughout his soul. 'I'm going to miss you when I go home tomorrow.' He couldn't begin to imagine not being beside her, shoulder to shoulder, thigh to thigh, as he went to sleep, or hand in hand as they walked along the riverbank, or— Stop. This wasn't doing any good for either of them.

She pulled away. 'Goodnight, Blake.' She turned and walked out of the room.

Out of his life for ever? No. He couldn't handle that. He loved her. 'Georgie,' he called.

She didn't hesitate, or look back, just continued down the hall to her bedroom.

And with every step she took, his heart cracked a little bit more. He loved her.

So go after her, pledge your heart to her and say you'll do whatever is necessary to keep her happy.

Was he absolutely certain of that? To love Georgie meant everything about him was committed to her. To do whatever it took to keep her happy and safe. And if they got it wrong? She'd said she hadn't loved her husband enough. What if the same happened with him? Or he found he couldn't let go the past enough to be able to be at her side throughout the journey of their lives? His heart dropped to his feet. So much to lose. For both of them.

'Goodnight, Georgie,' he whispered as he let himself out of the house.

His heart was heavy, his head aching. What if something bad happened? Not Georgie falling out of love with him—if she ever fell in love with him—but an accident or illness taking her away from him? What if it happened to him and she was on her own again? Could he live with that? He'd let so many people down when Noah died. By letting the guilt and fear wreck his life he'd hurt his family. He could not do that to Georgie.

He needed time out. Time on his own to do some serious thinking. That's how he operated best. Alone with nobody to intrude upon his thoughts. It was when he was most honest with himself. He'd just spent nearly four weeks surrounded by Georgie and his family. He hadn't been that amongst people for a long time. He needed space. Alone time.

But first he had a board meeting tomorrow that he'd given his word he'd attend.

Then he'd work out what he was going to do. Though he was already halfway there.

Leaving Georgie, hearing her front door click shut behind him, had hit him in the heart. There were major things to sort out before he could lay his heart on the line because, when he did, it had to be without any problems hanging over him.

The week was endless. Every night after work, Georgie mowed lawns, weeded the garden, cleaned the house and thought about Blake nonstop. Most mornings she arrived at the hospital far too early and filled in an hour before her first patient arrived for surgery drinking copious quantities of tea and wondering how she was going to get through the coming weeks.

Blake either loved her or he didn't. Seemed to her, he didn't. He hadn't got in contact, but neither had she called him, hoping that by giving him space that would work in her favour. He'd said he'd miss her. Big deal. She was missing him as she would an amputated leg. So the fling was over. Finished. As flings tended to do. But she'd fallen in love with him. So much for avoiding getting hurt again. This time seemed worse than the others. Far worse. Blake felt like her other half, the man to go through the rest of life with. To raise children with. To just be plain old happy with. It wasn't happening.

On Thursday morning Jane put her head around her office door. 'Megan Roper's at the desk. She had some bleeding overnight and is a bit frantic.'

Megan had had her third artificial insemination eight weeks ago, and had been on tenterhooks ever since. 'I'll see her straight away. And can you get me a mug of tea? I ran out of time this morning.'

'No problem. You sure you don't mean coffee though?'

Georgie shuddered at the thought. Which was bizarre. She loved coffee. 'Tea for a change.'

'Want a sandwich too? I'm presuming you didn't have time for anything to eat either.'

'Sounds good, thanks.' Blake had made toast for them both, but she'd left hers on the plate. She'd better not be coming down with a stomach bug. Not while Blake was still here. That time was for him, not lying in bed feeling unwell.

'Dr Price, I'm sorry to barge in without an appointment, but I can't lose another baby.' Megan stood in the doorway, pale and trembling. 'I can't.'

'You know I'm here whenever you need me. Come in and close the door, then tell me what's been going on.'

Georgie sat in her office and stared at her phone. Her hand rubbed her stomach lightly. As it had been doing often since Megan Roper left here that morning. The younger woman had been panicking over losing her baby, a fear Georgie recalled all too clearly. The sheer panic that disabled clear thinking, followed by the anguish and sense of failure, and then the grief. Hard, fast and debilitating, the grief was the worst.

Thankfully she'd been able to reassure Megan she wasn't miscarrying. The spotting was normal, but as the woman had already lost two babies through miscarriage she wasn't entirely convinced. Georgie could only offer time on that.

Time mightn't be on Georgie's side though. Not if her suspicions were right. How could they be when they had used condoms every single time they made love? Her stomach was tight, as were her chest and neck. She was making this up because it fit nicely into the picture of her and Blake and family. A picture he did not want. He'd been adamant about not being a father. He might've got close to her but children were still not on his radar. He hadn't said so after that one time, but he didn't need to. She had got the message loud and clear. She'd also felt he didn't love her. But hell, she loved him, and she would love their baby as she'd never loved before. She'd be devoted to him or her. Completely and utterly.

Now she was waiting for another message—from the lab this time. It had been a lightning bolt moment. Megan was leaving the office and the receptionist was walking towards Georgie with the sandwiches she'd offered to get for her, and she'd thought, 'That's why I couldn't face breakfast most mornings. I'm pregnant.' It would also explain why the wine had suddenly tasted sour the other night.

If she was pregnant it was very early for this to be happening, but she knew from her patients that what the books on pregnancy symptoms and timing spouted all went out the door more often than not. Last time she fell pregnant she hadn't been aware of it until she'd missed a second period, and even then she'd been dubious, thinking it couldn't happen when she and Tommy hadn't decided on being parents quite so soon. But the moment she'd seen the thin blue line on the stick she'd been in raptures, thinking that at last her life was getting back on its feet. Not a good idea to be remembering that. Take this one moment at a time. A result first.

She stared at the phone. It was silent. Far too silent.

She should call Blake. He'd support her as she waited. Her hand shook as she reached for her personal phone. Stop. That was the last thing she should be doing. If Blake knew, he'd be hoping for a negative result. While she— Did she want a baby? She'd always hoped that one day she'd have moved on and be able to try again, but that meant being in a relationship with someone. That someone now had a name, a loving face, a mind she adored. Blake. Now it was too late to be wondering if she wanted a baby. She either was or wasn't, and if she was, then yes, it would be wonderful and she'd love

him or her to bits. To hell with everything
else. She was over holding back on loving.

Leaning back in her chair, she stared out
the window at the newly weeded gardens.
Until she heard from the lab she wasn't
going anywhere.

The phone vibrated.

Snatching it up, she stared at the screen.

The message read: Georgina Price HCG
45mIU/ml.

She was pregnant. She and Blake were
going to be parents. It was too much. She
needed to talk to somebody, and the only
person she wanted was Blake. Nor could it
be anyone else. It wasn't as though she could
mention the pregnancy to someone before
he knew. How was he going to take the news
when it was the last thing he ever wanted?

He needed to know.

She had to tell him. But this wasn't something to do over the phone. She had to be
there, see his reactions, know what he was
thinking. That meant flying to Auckland
and knocking on his door to tip his world
upside down. At least she could hold his
hand while she did that.

She stared at the result on the screen. A

storm of emotion poured through her. She was pregnant. A baby to love. Someone to give her heart to without any restrictions. Tears streamed down her cheeks. This had to be one of the best days of her life. If only Blake was here to share in the news, to enjoy it as much as she was.

She had to share the news, no matter how he took it. No matter that she wasn't in front of him. She knew his voice, his nuances, she'd know how he felt. Her thumb banged the phone, brought up Blake's number, pushed Dial.

His voice mail answered. He must be having a busy day at work.

She hit Stop. No way was she giving Blake this news in a message. This had to be dealt with face to face. She'd fly up on Saturday after her rounds in the morning.

Once at home, Georgie made a ham sandwich, pulled out her laptop and typed in 'gynaecologist positions in Auckland,' then held her breath as the screen filled up with headings leading to advertisements for jobs. It looked promising until she began going through them and found there were very few opportunities in the big city.

Relief had her clicking out of the screen. She really didn't want to go there. It would be hard to start at the bottom of the ladder again. But if Blake didn't want to move back here, then she'd consider it for their child's sake, at least.

If she carried it to full term. A chill settled over her, as it did at least once a day as memories of her miscarriage rose. They rattled her like nothing else could. She wanted this baby. Loved it already. If she lost it, she had no idea how she'd get beyond that.

Blake, I love you. All of you. The best bits, and the not so great ones, like when you hog all the sheets or leave your dirty coffee mug on the table when you leave the house.

If only she'd told him that before she walked away, leaving him standing in her kitchen looking bewildered that last night. He'd have laughed.

Now Georgie laughed for the first time in days. He did that to her when she wasn't being all uptight about what they were going to do.

Blake, I'm coming up to see you on Saturday, and you'd better be prepared for life-changing news.

* * *

On Friday afternoon, Georgie helped deliver twins, but they didn't lift her spirits as they normally would've. All she felt was sadness at what she and Blake were missing out on. Especially Blake. She was pregnant and he wasn't here. Not that she looked any different yet. And it was too early for baby to kick. But she was carrying his child, and she was certain he'd want to be a part of its life, even when he'd sworn he'd never be a father. Hopefully he'd want to be a part of hers too. She headed outside to go home and pack her overnight bag.

Outside in the carpark, her phone rang. Blake.

Her heart jerked. 'Hi.' Where had all the things she wanted to tell him gone? Her mouth was dry as a desert and her tongue too big for her mouth. 'Blake?' she squeaked.

'Georgie, sorry I haven't called earlier. It's been hectic up here and I've had little time to spare.'

'I did wonder if you'd gone silent on me. But it's all right. I don't want to lose touch.'

That's everything.

She could try begging him to give their

relationship a chance, but she didn't do begging. Never had and wasn't about to start.

'We're not going to.' He sounded fierce, like it was the most important thing for him.

'Good.' Because she was going up to see him tomorrow. 'Are you busy over the weekend?' Should she share her news now? Then when she got to Auckland he'd have had time to absorb all the implications?

'Yes, I am. Oh, damn, sorry, Georgie. I've got to go. Take care. Talk again soon.'

The call ended.

'What? Hello, Blake. Don't call me only to hang up suddenly. Talk again soon. Not if I see you coming.' Her patience evaporated in an instant, if it had been there in the first place. Punching Blake's number again, she got the bland voice saying to leave a message. She snapped, 'Don't shut me out, Blake. I deserve better than that. So do you.' Her hand holding the phone lifted above her shoulder, aimed at the furthest wall. Two deep breaths and she lowered it. 'Damn you. Blake Newman. I love you, and that has to be good for both of us.'

Moving to Auckland might not be an option after all if Blake wasn't going to be available some of the time. She'd be alone, new job, new house, new baby. She shook her head. He said he was busy. On a late Friday afternoon? Well, it did happen. She knew that, but why phone when there was every chance he'd be called away? Was she being fair? He didn't know she was pregnant. Not yet. Tomorrow he might have a different opinion about everything.

She'd become entrenched in Christchurch. Most of her history was here. There'd been a time when she planned on moving away, and then she'd used her family as an excuse to cancel that dream, and had continued to do so whenever anything risky came into her life. A picture came to mind of her mother's excitement about the enormous campervan they bought a few months ago. She'd been thrilled to think they'd be able to go on holidays up and down the country without having to plan ahead. They hadn't gone far afield yet, and only for a couple of nights as they both had to go to work. But retirement loomed for both of them once summer was out, and they were adamant they'd hit the road then. Go north for a warm winter, take in the sights and enjoy the various golf courses on the way. No, they didn't need her hanging around, being at their beck and call. They had moved on, and were enjoying everything that came their way.

Not like her. She loved her work, and had believed she wouldn't change it for anything. But now there was a hollow inside her that was waiting to be filled with love and laughter, with a partner and children. She had moved beyond the fear of being crushed again by losing someone she loved, and had immediately fallen in love with the man who'd helped do that. So shouldn't she be helping Blake move beyond his demons too? Here, or in Auckland, it didn't really matter where as long as they were together. If he wanted to be with her, that was. And wanted to be a father to their baby.

Blake dropped into his allocated seat, buckled his seatbelt and stared out at the runway. Georgie had left a message on his phone. She was spitting mad and he didn't blame her, but he'd thought he'd have a few minutes to talk to her before the taxi reached the terminal. Now he'd have to placate her when he arrived at her house. Hopefully she'd give him a few minutes of her time so he could explain what he'd been doing since he'd left her last week.

Work had been hectic which usually made him grateful for keeping the gremlins at bay, but there'd been so many other things needing his attention he'd been frustrated all week. Odd how he hadn't felt comfortable in his house since he'd returned from Christchurch and left Georgie behind. It felt large and gloomy, lonely with no laughter to tighten his groin and soften his heart. These past days the stream of patients and surgeries had only frustrated him further and had him realising he didn't really want to stay in Auckland following his dream career if it meant not being a part of Georgie's life. He was still afraid of what could go wrong and the pain that would inflict on both of them, but especially he didn't want her hurt. He was ready to step up and take the chance with Georgie. Otherwise what was he doing with his life? Why bother with his career if he couldn't share the highs and low with her? Why get the house looking wonderful and all comfortable if he only used the kitchen, bathroom, lounge and one bedroom? It sounded hollow after the nights he'd spent in Georgie's.

Hell, nothing had been the same since the moment Georgie walked into the clinic where his mother was seeing her specialist. From that moment on he'd been fighting a losing battle to keep his heart safe. Not that he'd tried too hard, had given in to the need she cranked up in him with little more than a glance. And when that glance came with a gut-clenching smile, then he was a goner in all ways imaginable.

He loved her. He wasn't in love with her. He loved her outright. No ifs, buts or maybes.

So what was he going to do about it?

First, he was walking away from his partnership.

He was going to be happy for the first time in years. Make that, continue to be happy as he had been with Georgie.

Become a regular part of his family again.

Add to that family by marrying Georgie, if she'd have him.

Then there was the big one that still made

him suck a breath whenever he thought about it. He wanted to have a child with her. Maybe not quite yet. Too soon. They could enjoy getting to know each other even better.

Georgie or Auckland? He'd made the decision. Simple as that. He would not ask her to move up here when she was settled where she was. Far more settled than he was, really.

The fact was he struggled to get through every day without her. The decision had been made weeks ago without him realising, and not seeing her, or holding her, was driving him crazy. Love was a damned thing. It grabbed your heart and sure as hell had no intention of letting go.

He leaned back and closed his eyes and waited for the plane to depart Auckland.

A little over an hour later Blake stared down through the small window as Christchurch City came into view. Home. The place he'd been born and raised, had gone to school and met the best mate any guy could ever hope for. The city had expanded and altered in the years he'd been away and it felt a bit like how he was feeling about himself really. Old but new. Strong but desperate to make a change. To start over. The hang-ups from the past had gone, and he could move forward with a lightness in his heart he hadn't known for a long time, if ever.

All because of Georgie. Who'd have believed it? He would've, if he'd ever stopped to think about it. About her. It was as easy as downing a glass of water to recall how his blood used to heat at the sight of her when he was a teen. Back then he had known instinctively he didn't have a chance of getting close to her. She was his best mate's sister. She was also a few years older and wouldn't have seen him as anything but the teenager he was. He'd known to keep his thoughts to himself. As he'd got on with living and studying and becoming an adult he'd somehow managed to put those feelings aside to the point he believed he had forgotten about Georgie as anyone more than Noah's sister, someone to ask for information about aspects of campus once he'd started his university degree.

Had he ever really got over those feelings for her? Or had he buried them along with all the other emotions that took over when Noah died? More than likely that was the truth of it. Otherwise why had he reacted so positively to Georgie so fast? It had been as though his body had been waiting for her to reappear in his life. Come on. Body? It was his heart mostly affected here. His heart had never been so involved with another person.

Which had nothing to do with Georgie and how he felt about her. Or did it? His heart was so tied to her he couldn't imagine life without her at his side, pushing him to be the best he could at anything he attempted. She wouldn't let him down, wouldn't say he wasn't good enough for her—because he'd make damned sure he was.

You left her behind in Christchurch. Walked away as if there could be no future with her.

Yes, he had, because he had to be absolutely certain he was doing the right thing by both of them. It hadn't taken long to know he couldn't live without Georgie. Now he was heading back, hoping to convince her he loved her and wanted to spend the rest of his life with her. Now he understood that life did crush people, hurt them beyond measure sometimes, and when that happened he'd be there for Georgie no matter what. She was special, deserved love and kindness and caring, and not being let down. And she'd made him whole again. Hopefully he could do the same for her.

She was his heart.

Blake checked his safety belt was buckled, and leaned back in the upright seat, closing his eyes to breathe deep as he waited for the plane to touch down.

Damn, how he'd missed Georgie's smile. Her beautiful face. That long, silky hair that slipped through his fingers. He missed the softening in his heart whenever she was near, or right up close, pressing that divine body into his. But most of all, he'd missed that smile. It got to him every single time she wore it.

Less than four weeks was all it had taken to tip his world upside down. Nearly four weeks of sun-kissed days and nights. Georgie-kissed hours of pleasure and excitement. Days of talking, sharing points of view on politics and medicine, disagreeing on car models and fishing. Ordinary days that were filled with love, and amazement that he could have so much fun with one person.

Ka-thump. The plane was on the ground.

He'd come home. Now all he had to do was convince Georgie to give him a chance. He loved her. Did she love him? There'd been something like love in her eyes when they'd been calling it quits on their fling. She wanted all or nothing. Well, he was about to offer her everything.

A car door slammed, making Georgie sit back in her seat on the deck and look towards the drive. Who'd come to visit? Her parents were still away, and her girlfriend was on duty in the ER.

The hairs on her arms began to rise. Could it be? No, it couldn't. He hadn't returned her calls, apart from that one abrupt time. Settle down, heart. He wasn't coming back.

Blake came around the corner of the house and into her befuddled view.

Blake. What was he doing here? Her mouth dried as the blood in her veins drained into a pool somewhere low in her body. Her hand spread across her still flat stomach. 'Blake.' He was stunning. So good-looking her skin heated. But then she was biased. Her dream come true stood before her, holding out his hands to her, while she was kneeling down here like a stuffed toy, unable to move for fear she'd wake from the dream to find nothing but chilly autumn air in front of her.

'Hello, Georgie.' He stepped closer and reached for her hands, tugged her gently to her feet. 'Thought I'd pay you a visit. Without warning,' he added around a hopeful smile. 'I didn't want to be turned away.'

Just as well he was holding her or she'd be in a heap in the vegetable patch. 'I'd never turn you away. You have no idea how I feel seeing you standing there. Oh, my message on your phone. Sorry, I was peeved you couldn't talk for longer. Now, I'm over that. You're not getting away for at least the next hour.' Her smile felt crooked and there might be a smattering of tears in her eyes, but her back was ramrod straight, and her chin had a determined angle to it. He had come back. Why? For how long?

'I've missed you.' He stepped up to her and put his arms around her, and rubbed his chin over the top of her head. 'I've missed you so much it hurts.'

She pulled away. 'Slow down, Blake. I want to know what this is about.'

Tipping his head back so he could lock that steady grey gaze on her, he said clearly, 'I've come home, Georgie. To you. And yes, to my family also. But most of all to you. I know I've been aloof at times, but it has been hard to accept I can change, can move on, and I owe you for that.'

Her mouth fell open. It was what she'd been hoping for, but not expecting to happen. Not for a long while anyway. 'You're serious?' she whispered.

He dipped his head. 'I couldn't be more so. I haven't come for a one-night party. I've come for the whole deal. I love you. To the moon and back. Everything about you. I love you, Georgie.'

Her heart soared. Blake was serious about this. About him and them. As serious as she was. 'Blake, I love you too. I nearly told you the other night, but I got cold feet, thinking you'd run.'

'Which I sort of did.' His arms tightened around her. 'When I said I'd been busy, it wasn't only work keeping me on my feet. I've given up my partnership and have put the house on the market. I mean it when I say I'm coming home. Even more serious about loving you.' His mouth found hers. His kiss sent a thrill down her back, and into her heart, touched her toes and a lot of places in between.

Blake had come back for her, to be with her. Georgie pulled back. There was more news to share. It could be a deal-breaker, but from that genuine look of love in his eyes she was starting to doubt that. He looked so happy, as happy as she felt.

'I'd crawl to the other side of the world and back if it'd make you happy.' He was smiling. He meant what he said.

'You don't have to go that far.' Warmth stole through her, around their baby he knew nothing about. 'Come inside.'

He followed her in and closed the door behind them. 'I've missed this place, being here with you. I have finally found what I didn't know I was looking for.'

She pinched herself, then him. 'When do you finish at the practice?' she asked to give herself a moment to get her thoughts together. This news could be a deal-breaker.

'I've got to work for another two months

and then I start down here at Orthopaedics United. The two months give the partners time to find a suitable replacement. And me time to pack up, and make plans down here, hopefully with you.'

Okay, here we go.

'Blake, before we go any further, there's something you need to know.' Deep inhale. 'I'm pregnant.'

He looked as though someone was shining a headlight into his face. Good? Or bad? 'You're what?'

'Having our baby.' She picked up her phone and scrolled through the messages until the lab report popped up. 'I had the test done last week.'

His eyes dropped to the screen, but he didn't take the phone from her. He blinked, stared some more, a smile creeping across his face, lightening his eyes. 'You *are* pregnant.'

This had to be good. Surprisingly good.

'Wow. I mean, who'd have thought when we were so careful. Blimey.' He was still staring at the screen. 'We're having a baby,' he shouted. Then he picked her up in his arms and swung her around. 'This is getting better and better by the minute. This is the best news after hearing you love me. I thought we might try, just not so soon.'

'No trying needed.' Laughter fought with relief bubbling throughout her body as the last drop of tension left her. Blake was okay with the pregnancy, more than okay. He was as thrilled as she was. 'I can't wait to meet him or her.'

He was grinning at her. 'I'm stunned, but I'm also excited. I can't believe how happy your news makes me. I came here to tell you I love you, and to ask you to marry me, and now this. I did say I couldn't cope with the idea of children, but neither would I have believed a few weeks ago that I'd fall in love with you and want the whole picture.' He was pulling her up against him, placing kisses on her cheeks, her throat, her mouth.

This was what she'd missed so much. She kissed back with all the love in her heart.

His mouth lifted from hers just enough for him to say, 'I love you, Georgie.' Then he went back to kissing her. He was serious about being with her. Really serious. She threw her arms around his neck and held him tight. Made her kisses longer, deeper, and felt as though she was the one who'd finally come home.

Suddenly he pulled back, still holding her but looking into her eyes. 'I meant what I said. Will you marry me, Georgie Price?'

'You bet.' Her whole body had gone so soft with love it was hard to stand upright. 'I love you too, and want more than anything to be Mrs Newman.'

His smile went right to her toes. 'Thank goodness. I love you, Georgie. I always have and I always will.'

It couldn't get any better than that. She leapt into his arms. 'Yes, yes, yes. I love you, Blake, so yes.' Her lips found his and she kissed him as though her life depended upon it. Which it did.

When they finally came up for air, she grinned. 'So you're returning home at last. Think you'd like to move in with me?'

'I'd love to move in with you, starting right now. I'll be a commuter for a while, but as of now this is officially my home address along with my fiancée.'

Georgie rubbed her tummy lightly. 'You hear that, baby? Daddy's coming home.'

Blake looked away, wiped his eyes,

turned back. 'I love you beyond measure. Why did it take so long to figure it all out?'

'Guess that's how it was meant to be.' And now the zip was closed right to the last click. The past hadn't gone away, but it was done with ruining the future. She was so happy her chest ached. So damned happy she had to pinch herself.

Blake's smile was so wide it had to ache. 'Let's not take too long to tie the knot. You seemed ready to commit before I was, and now I don't want to waste any more time.'

'I had reached the point where I couldn't go on with the fling, but I didn't want to lose you either. It was the hardest thing hearing you leave that night, but I couldn't run after you and demand you stay. You had to be ready.'

'I am. Totally.'

Seven months later, message on Georgie and Blake Newman's web page

To all our family and friends—Jacob Noah Newman arrived four hours ago, checking in at six and a half pounds. He's healthy and already has a cheeky grin. Wonder where he gets that from? Georgie's looking great, but then, when doesn't she? Me? I'm ecstatic beyond description. Never knew I could be so happy.

Blake. X

Oh, and yes, I love these two so much it hurts, and I can cope with that.

* * * * *

If you enjoyed this story, check out these other great reads from Sue MacKay

Their Second Chance in ER
From Best Friends to I Do?
A Single Dad to Rescue Her
Captivated by the Runaway Doc

All available now!